ONE
NIGHT
IN
NOVEMBER

ALSO BY AMÉLIE ANTOINE

Interference

ONE NIGHT IN NOVEMBER

Amélie Antoine

Translated by Maren Baudet Lackner

amazon crossing

Text copyright © 2016 Amélie Antoine
Translation copyright © 2017 Maren Baudet-Lackner

Previously published as *Au nom de quoi* by Amélie Antoine in 2016 in France. Translated from French by Maren Baudet-Lackner. First published in English by AmazonCrossing in 2017.

Published by AmazonCrossing, Seattle
www.apub.com

ISBN-13: 9781503942608
ISBN-10: 1503942600

Cover design by Rex Bonomelli

Printed in the United States of America

To all those who were there.
And to all those who were not.

Le deuil n'existe pas. On se souvient. On se souviendra toujours de tout. Dans les moindres détails.

There is no mourning. We remember. We will remember it all. Down to the last detail.

—Bertrand Betsch

I

Before

1

Abigaëlle

"There's no need to stomp up the stairs! The only person you should be mad at is yourself."

I spin around to glare at my mother, who is standing at the bottom of the stairs with arms crossed, triumphant and sure of herself. The furious snort that puffs suddenly out of my nose sends a strand of my hair flying. I'm livid and refuse to look away as a silent staring contest gets under way between us.

"Do you even know how much I paid for my ticket?"

"Do you expect me to care, Abi? The only things that matter are your grades, studying for the baccalaureate practice test, and your career plans. In other words, everything you find useless."

"That's all there is to life for you. School, school, school! God, Mom, that's not what really counts! It's like you were never a teenager, like you don't even know what it means to have fun and relax."

My mother shakes her head disdainfully.

"Relax? At seventeen you already need to 'relax'? You poor dear. Please tell me what has you so stressed out. What party you'll be invited to next? The next dress you absolutely must buy? Explain it to me, because I don't understand . . ."

"As usual. You don't understand anything."

I turn around wearily and finish climbing the stairs to my room. I plug my ears to block out my mother's chiding and kick my door shut as hard as I can. The framed photo on the wall falls to the ground, seemingly as disgusted as I am.

I hurry to hang it back up on its nail, perfectly straight, and run my finger over my best friend Clara's face. The photo was taken in our high school courtyard last summer. One of her blonde dreads is perched under my nose like a mustache, and she's holding a thick strand of my brown mane to her chin like a beard. Yet another ridiculous pose—it's what we always do whenever someone takes our picture.

Clara's been my best friend since we were little, but she's so much more than that. She's my confidante, my ally, my twin. We know everything about one another; we haven't kept a secret from each other since we became friends at the age of four, when her family moved into the house next door. The first time I saw her was in our backyards. I still remember it clearly, even though my mother says there's no way I could have any memories from that age. Clara was wearing a teal anorak with white fur trim on the hood. It fell over her eyes as she played in the dirt, squatting down to focus her attention on an earthworm squirming at the end of a stick she was holding. I said, "Yuck," out of disgust and curiosity, and she wordlessly passed me the stick through the fence between our yards.

That's how our friendship began: with an earthworm. We quickly fell into the habit of getting together after school to play catch, trade toys, or just tell each other about our lives, even if our discussions must have seemed trivial to adults.

After a few weeks, our parents cut a large rectangular hole in the fence that separated Clara and me. The two yards became one, and so did we, in a way. Everyone called us "Clara-N-Abi," as if we were a single entity, a single person. Over the years, no other child managed to break up our inseparable duo, even when we were in different classes.

In elementary school, we could hardly wait for recess; in middle school, it was the time between classes and lunch.

And now that we're in high school, sometimes we don't even wait for passing periods—we just skip school. When it's warm, we hide behind a little hill in the school courtyard and lie in the thinning grass to smoke in secret. In the winter, we take refuge in the bathrooms, huddled against the radiator as we share the week's gossip and talk about the guys we've got our eyes on, and the ones who are getting a little too friendly. Clara's always chewing gum, and our discussions are regularly interrupted by bubbles popping and the sticky paste she pulls quickly off her nose.

Clara is an awesome friend and so laid-back. When I found out on Facebook that Ilan was going to the Eagles of Death Metal concert with his friends, she immediately agreed to come with me. Ilan is the senior guy I've been crushing on for a few months now. I wasn't able to get close to him last year, but that's because I was only a sophomore. Now that I'm a junior, I know there's a chance he might look at me differently; I'm not a little girl anymore. I just need to find the right time to talk to him, to show him how cool I am, that we have things in common. A rock concert will be perfect. I've been listening to the band's latest albums on repeat for three months now so I can show him I'm a real fan, even if I'd never heard of them before this summer. I've even started memorizing the words to the most popular songs.

All we have to do is find him at the concert. The Bataclan isn't that big, so it shouldn't be too hard. Clara and I will pretend we've run into him and his friends by accident, and that'll be that. He'll say, *Wow, I had no idea you listened to this kind of music!* and I'll reply with as much nonchalance as I can manage, *Are you kidding? I've already been to, like, three concerts. These guys are so amaaaazing.* Maybe I'll even ask Clara for a piece of gum to really fit in. I definitely don't want Ilan to know it's my first concert.

Anyway, that's the plan I've been hatching since the first day of school. Because I hadn't expected my mom to ground me for getting a C in math. What good is math anyway? I'm on the literary track for a reason, aren't I?

Snuggled up in my comforter, I dial Clara's number. She picks up on the first ring, like always.

"It's me. My mom just told me I can't go to the concert tomorrow night."

"She's a real pain in the ass, that one. Did you tell her that we'd already bought the tickets and that they weren't cheap?"

"She doesn't care. You know how she is."

"So that's it, then?"

"Are you kidding? She didn't even ask me for the tickets; she's too mad to think straight. We'll just meet at Oberkampf. I won't come home after school."

"Works for me. You're not worried about the fallout?"

"I just think it's worth being grounded for another two weeks."

"You must really be in looove, then!"

"I'm putting the odds in my favor, that's all."

"Suuure. Seven thirty at the Metro stop, then?"

"Perfect."

I hang up with a smile and go open my closet. A jean dress with a black rhinestone belt will be perfect with my fitted leather jacket and a dark-blue wool beanie with metallic threads woven in for extra sparkle. It's not really cold enough for hats yet, but I know it looks really good on me, and that's what counts.

And turquoise tights, obviously.

I type a message on my smartphone at lightning speed: Wear turquoise tights, ok? Barely a second later, the answer arrives: Will do!

Clara and I have been wearing matching tights since we were little. It's kind of our lucky charm.

My mother knocks softly on my door, then cracks it open cautiously, as if afraid I might throw a grenade at her face. "Can we talk for a few minutes, please?"

I put on the sullenest face possible and sit back on my bed. I squeeze my pillow tightly in my arms. Here's hoping the lecture will be short and sweet.

2

PHILIPPE

The semi is hurtling toward me at what must be seventy miles an hour. I tighten my grip on the bridge's guardrail as I look down at the highway. I lean my whole body forward until I can feel the metal bar almost under my ribs. The wind is howling in my ears, and I have to yell as loud as I can for Pascal to hear me.

"Lean over more! Lean like you're going to jump, and make sure to look down!"

My friend and former colleague doubtfully lowers his head toward the asphalt and the roofs of the cars zooming by. At last, the semi passes under the bridge, under us, and for a fraction of a second, the breath is knocked out of me thanks to the incredible illusion that it's brushed past me at full speed, pulling me in its wake. I burst into laughter, while Pascal simply raises his head again, unimpressed.

"So, isn't it an incredible feeling when the truck goes past? Have you ever felt so . . . *alive*?"

"I dunno. Sorry, man, I must not have focused on it enough, but it's nice of you to try."

I sigh disappointedly.

"We can try again. It's not like there's any shortage of trucks."

Pascal shakes his head. "No, that's all right."

I study his drawn features, the dark circles under his tired eyes, the corners of his mouth turned slightly downward. I'm almost certain they didn't slump sadly like that before.

Before, meaning before he got fired eight months ago. Pascal and I were colleagues for a dozen or so years, long enough for him to become more a friend than a colleague—part of my family, even. The brother I'd always wished for, as my wife would say. We used to both be bus drivers, but now only I am. I don't even know how they chose who to let go. *Layoffs for financial reasons*, they told us. *Nobody's fault, simply bad luck. Not enough passengers to be profitable, so we're shutting down lines and we have to let drivers go too.* That's what they said. So they crossed Pascal off the roster, randomly, I guess. It could just as easily have been me.

Pascal often says, "When you've driven a bus your whole life, what else can you do?" And, well, I don't know what to say, since I already feel awkward about being kept on. "Why me?" he asks, and all I can do is shake my head and sigh that life's not fair. Not fair at all.

Now and then he finds a temp job doing inventory in clothing or big-box stores, but I know he feels out of place. "It's a bunch of kids and they look at me like . . . like they hope they won't still be there when they're my age . . ." I tell him there's nothing to be ashamed of, nothing at all.

I try to help him think about other things. Because I can see that he's depressed, that he's got the blues from sitting around doing nothing and expecting nothing. I can tell it drives him crazy to have to go to the unemployment office, that it makes him feel hopeless to realize he may never find another job and that he'll have to keep living off his wife's paycheck. I can tell he's restless, that it's driving him nuts to want something so badly and not be able to make it happen, to feel capable while being the only one who thinks he's good for anything. He even tells anyone who'll listen to take the bus; after all, he reasons, it might just create a need for drivers. Then maybe the company would think of him.

So we have a beer together after my shift; he comes to dinner at my place on the weekend with his wife. I take him to soccer games, try to find things to make him happy. Watching the trucks go by didn't work, but other things do. I know Pascal. He's a fighter. He's going through a rough patch, but it won't last. I mostly just want him to know he can count on me, that I won't write him off.

"I've got a surprise for you!"

"Oh yeah?"

Pascal doesn't seem very interested, but I'm enthusiastic enough for the both of us.

"I managed to get us two tickets to a great concert! On Friday, you and I are going on a little road trip to Paris, if you're available."

"I'm always available, you know that . . ."

It takes more than that to make me give up.

"Great. The drive takes a little over an hour, so we'll leave late afternoon. Try to be a bit more excited because let me tell you, it wasn't easy to rustle up these tickets!"

I'm not exaggerating either. The concert had been sold out for a while, and I'd scoured the ads for weeks to find someone who'd sell two tickets without trying to line his pockets as part of the deal. Monday night, I met up with the guy I'd been looking for—a certain Simon—in front of Gare du Nord. An hour each way just to get the tickets! It was easy to pick him out of the crowd: a wannabe rocker around thirty, with black jeans with holes in the knees, a black leather jacket, and sunglasses hooked onto his sweater collar, though there wasn't the slightest glimmer of sunshine anywhere. I handed him the money for the tickets, but I could tell it was painful for him to let them go. Given his long face, I tried to seem interested.

"So why are you selling them anyway?"

"I was supposed to go with someone . . . but it fell through."

"Oh . . . I'm sorry to hear that."

Thinking about the hour-long train ride home, I slipped the tickets into my inner jacket pocket and started to move away, but the guy kept talking. He must have needed to get his feelings off his chest; they were clearly weighing on him.

"I actually bought the tickets for my girlfriend. But she broke up with me last weekend, so I don't really feel like going anymore."

"I understand . . . Don't worry, there are plenty of fish in the sea!"

He made a pained face, a bit like the one my son makes when he's embarrassed of me, so I quickly and awkwardly added, "Or maybe your girlfriend will ask you to get back together! You never know with women . . ."

He nodded half-heartedly—undoubtedly blown away by such polished philosophy and in-depth knowledge of womankind—and I hurriedly disappeared into the station and down the escalator to the suburban trains.

Seriously, though. I worked hard to get these tickets!

Pascal finally smiles.

"It's nice of you to take your old pal out on the town."

"Stop acting like it's such a chore for me! I've been dying for months to go to a real rock concert. And don't tell me you won't enjoy a chance to shake your legs out a little!"

"Next to all those kids, we'll look like grandpas . . ."

"Well, we'll show them that you can still like good music at nearly fifty years old."

A semi passes under the bridge and I hurry to lean over the guard-rail. The swoosh of air seems to yank me along behind it.

"Woo-hoo! Seriously, man, you don't know what you're missing! It's an incredible feeling!"

Pascal bursts into laughter and gives me a firm slap on the back. I stifle the urge to tell him that I hate it when he does that; this is no time to be a killjoy.

◆ ◆ ◆

When I get home, the smell of the homemade paella simmering in the kitchen makes my mouth water.

"I'm home!"

I hastily take off my jacket and hang it on the coat rack as my son, Félix, mopes past me. He stares at me furiously as he heads toward the dining room.

"Come on, Félix, don't tell me you're still mad about the concert!"

He shrugs, refusing to dignify the question with an answer.

"I could only get two tickets, okay? Pascal really needs something to cheer him up right now. Don't you get that? Please? I'll take you next time, promise . . . !"

3

Sofiane

"Let me get this straight: you remember the date the tickets go on sale, sit in front of your computer on the big day feverishly pressing F5 to be the first to buy your ticket, lovingly stash it in your nightstand so you don't lose it, go through your collection of their T-shirts to carefully select the one best suited to the momentous occasion, waste twenty minutes meticulously ironing a neon-green skull, and all that doesn't even include the hour and a half you'll spend on various trains actually getting to this concert?"

Héloïse pauses to catch her breath midtirade. I know all too well that it's far from over.

"But you can't even spend an hour of your precious time helping me plan the wedding that's only three months away? *Our* wedding?"

My future wife crosses her arms over her chest; I know her well enough to realize she expects an answer. Though I'm aware that nothing I say will make me look any better in her eyes, I mumble something, hoping to assuage her anger a bit.

"You know how much I love this band. I've never missed one of their concerts—"

"Exactly! You already saw them at Rock en Seine a few years ago and at Le Trianon this summer. I don't understand why you need to go again tonight! They're not gods! Can't you just put in one of their CDs and crank the volume all the way up once in a while?"

I know that what I'm about to say won't help, but I can't stop myself.

"But you agreed it was okay when I bought the tickets this summer! It wasn't a problem then! It's not fair to make it into a big deal the night of—"

"Not fair?"

Héloïse echoes my words. I can already tell I should have opted for a different approach: the penitent boyfriend who apologizes to avoid being late and promises anything to prevent the conflict from escalating.

"Do you think it's fair that I spend all my evenings working on the invitations, sealing envelopes, writing addresses, planning the menu, finding a caterer, making table decorations, choosing music . . . Need I go on?"

I hunch a bit, instinctively. I need to sweet-talk her. I can see she's about to explode.

"I know you spend a ton of time on our wedding, and that I should help you out more often, but we still have three months left to perfect the finishing touches—"

"Perfect the finishing touches?"

I sigh. Apparently, I've said something stupid again. *Think before you speak,* my father used to whisper when I was younger and my mother was fuming about the dishes piling up in the sink.

"When all I have left to do is 'perfect the finishing touches,' I'll be relieved, believe me! Tonight I'm making little gift bags for the favors. I'm going to spend hours folding origami envelopes, then filling each of them with ten white candied almonds and four silver-coated chocolate drops. In other words, an awesome evening's ahead!"

I want to suggest that we not hand out favors to our guests, but a sudden stroke of genius dissuades me from voicing the idea to my fiancée.

"And tomorrow night I'm going to pull out my hair over the seating chart, figuring out who to sit next to whom so that everyone's happy. My grandparents, who can't stand my uncle Michel; your mother, who will want to be as far as possible from your father; my cousin Ludivine, who will want to sit across from her boyfriend rather than next to him because 'It's easier to talk that way!' Hours and hours of hassle, and, in the end, no one will be happy anyway. Oh, and my brother will probably switch all the place cards around secretly to play the world's funniest practical joke on me."

Defeated, I sit on the couch next to Héloïse. I hate to admit it, but I get why she's had enough of these endless preparations. That's precisely the reason I've stayed out of it since the beginning, except when all I had to do was choose between two distinct options.

"How about this: I'll miss the opening act and just show up for the Eagles. That leaves me an hour and a half to become an expert in origami. And I'll be home by midnight, so I can put in another hour or two then."

Héloïse's shoulders relax and I hug her close.

"As for the seating chart, I'll take care of it. Anybody who's unhappy can come talk to me. I don't want you to worry about it; I don't even want you to see it before the big day. I mean, it'll never be good enough anyway, right?"

She smiles and rests her head in the hollow of my neck. "Thank you," she murmurs in a tone that is both relieved and weary.

"As for the music, there are plenty of great songs on the most recent Eagles of Death Metal album. I'm sure they'd be perfect to play as we're leaving the church . . ."

Héloïse lifts her head and frowns at me, trying to decide if I'm being serious or not.

"I guess it was too soon for a joke. Sorry."

She mumbles something unintelligible, and I realize I've gotten myself into a real mess with this seating chart stuff.

For the next hour and a half, I watch the living room clock out of the corner of my eye while toiling away folding purple squares of paper based on a pattern that's much too complicated for my clumsy fingers. I suggest to Héloïse that it might be more efficient to have me put the candies into the envelopes she's able to make in less than a minute, but she refuses to take pity on me.

At 7:25 p.m., she taps her watch, and I jump up from the couch like a kid who's just heard the recess bell.

"See you later. Good luck!"

"Have fun."

As I kiss her, I can tell her entire being is focused on the origami envelopes.

I dash down the stairs of our building, thinking odds are I'll be late. Undiscouraged, I run down the street all the way to the train station.

Bataclan, here I come!

4

BASTIEN

Like almost every other Saturday since the beginning of September, at around noon, my bus pulls into the neighborhood where I grew up. The sun is shining in Rouen, and it occurs to me that I would have been more comfortable in a T-shirt than in my black button-down.

I use my key to open the front door of my childhood home and notice that the kitchen table is already set for lunch. My mother is busy tasting the veal stew that must have been simmering since this morning. I walk over to give her a hug and a kiss. When she turns to face me, her smile is radiant.

"Hi, sweetheart. How was the train?"

"All right. I took advantage of the time to work on my contemporary history presentation."

I started my first year at Sciences Po in Paris this year. It didn't take me long to realize that while I had successfully sailed through high school without much effort, I was going to have to work a lot harder now if I wanted to be anywhere near the top of my class.

My mother and I sit down to eat. I blow gently on my first bite of meat.

"Do you have any plans for this weekend?"

"No, not really. Maybe a movie tonight, if Arnaud is free. But I don't even know what's showing."

My mother keeps quiet, but I can tell from the look on her face that she's pleased at the idea of having her beloved son all to herself until tomorrow night.

"I might go see Dad this afternoon, lend a hand."

My father runs a butcher shop downtown—a family business for two generations, as he likes to remind everyone. All that really means is that he took over his father's shop; no big deal. But that doesn't lessen his pride in the least. I've always helped him on the weekends, serving customers or arranging the display case. But since September, I haven't been able to because I've been a bit overwhelmed by school. Now that I've found my rhythm, though, I'm looking forward to helping my father on the weekends again.

My mother puts her silverware down next to her plate and sighs.

"Bastien, I'm not sure that's a good idea. You know your father might feel awkward if you show up at the shop. And there are always so many customers on Saturdays . . ."

"Yes, and . . . ?"

I keep pushing, even though I know exactly what she's hinting at. I make her say the words, hoping that once she says them out loud she'll realize just how ridiculous they are.

"Do you really want to embarrass him?"

"Why would a visit from his only son embarrass him, Mom?"

She wrings her hands anxiously.

"You know why . . ."

"Because I'm gay? Because he's afraid that everyone will know, as if it were tattooed on my forehead?"

"He just needs some time to accept it, Bastien. Put yourself in his shoes—"

"Why does he need time? You're perfectly fine with me being gay. Why can't he see that I didn't change overnight, that I'm still the same person I always was, that the only difference is that now he *knows*?"

"He just needs to get used to it, that's all. Please don't get all worked up about it—"

"He's had all summer to 'get used to it'! It's been almost three months since he's spoken to me! He's so distant. He barely looks at me—he practically avoids me! Doesn't he know this is the twenty-first century? That homosexuality is neither a disease nor a choice?"

As usual, my mother defends her husband, even though I know she doesn't understand his behavior and is just as hurt as I am by his reactionary attitude.

"Look, it's hard for him. And then there's the fact that he was counting on you to take over the shop, to expand the deli and catering side of the business. It was a real blow, when you told us you were going to college in Paris—"

"But, Mom, don't you realize that you must be the only parents on the face of the earth who are disappointed that their child is going to college, and a prestigious one at that? How can you compare Sciences Po with working in a butcher shop?"

She shakes her head disappointedly. We've barely touched our food, and now the stew is probably cold. I know she's thinking that this discussion could at least have waited until dessert, that we're wasting the stew.

"Your father feels like you've rejected us, like we're not good enough for you, like you're ashamed of us—"

"You've got to be kidding me! Now I've heard it all! I've rejected *him*, when he's the one who doesn't want the family fag to embarrass him in front of his customers?"

"Don't talk like that, Bastien. There's no need to be vulgar. Fine, go to the shop and work it out with your father. I'm done playing the go-between."

All of a sudden, I notice how weary my mother seems, and my anger evaporates just as quickly as it came on.

"I'm sorry, Mom. It's not your fault."

She nods sadly and gets up to put my bowl in the microwave.

"It won't be as good reheated . . ."

"It'll be delicious, no matter what, don't worry . . ."

When we're done eating, my mother lights a cigarette, takes an envelope out of her purse, and hands it to me. She's written my name on it and even decorated it with a gold bow she must have saved from one of last year's Christmas presents.

"What's this?"

"A present, to congratulate you on getting into college. I've been wanting to get you something, but with everything that's happened, I haven't had the time until now . . ."

I carefully open the envelope and find two concert tickets inside. Eagles of Death Metal, in three weeks, in Paris.

"I overheard you talking about it on the phone the other day, so I thought maybe . . . I hope you haven't already bought tickets?"

"No. Mom, this is so nice of you . . . I don't know what to say . . ."

"I got two. That way you can go with . . . whomever you choose."

"Thank you so much. You couldn't have thought of a better gift!"

She finally looks happy.

After weighing the pros and cons, I decide to head downtown to confront my dad. The bell rings merrily as I push through the heavy glass door and into the butcher shop. My father darts out of the cold room, always eager to welcome a customer. He freezes when he realizes it's only me, then goes back to drying his blood-stained hands with a towel that must have once been white, long ago.

"Oh, it's you."

I raise my eyebrows.

"Keen sense of observation you've got there, Dad."

He doesn't seem to notice my gibe. He's still wiping his hands, though they must be dry by now.

"I thought maybe you could use some help?"

He sizes me up with a contemplative glance. I hold his gaze. I'm just waiting for him to tell me to leave.

"I was thinking of making a batch of lasagna. It always sells fast on Saturday nights."

"Perfect! Lasagna is my specialty," I say as I head to the pantry for an apron.

As I walk past him, he looks curiously at the four hoops wrapped around the rim of my ear. I decide to ignore his disapproving face.

I spend an hour sautéing onions and meat for the sauce, then layering it between sheets of pasta. My father works at the counter next to me, cutting, trimming, and breaking bones. With every blow, I can't help but think I'm the one he's imagining under his giant cleaver.

He doesn't say a word, and I decide not to make it easy for him. The sound of the knife against the cutting board is the only sound heard for the rest of the afternoon.

5

LÉOPOLD

"Think you could drive? I was hoping to take advantage of the ride to practice. I'm still having a hard time with one part . . ."

Alexandre sighs at length but accepts the key I press into his hand.

"Why me?" he groans, frowning at Sylvain and Tiago, who are already comfortably seated in the backseat of the station wagon.

Without waiting for an answer, he settles behind the wheel, mumbling into his perfect hipster beard. I walk around the car to the passenger side and launch the metronome app on my iPhone before he's even turned the key in the ignition. I choose the tempo, and the regular beat fills the car. Closing my eyes, I start drumming a fast riff on my lap with my sticks, ignoring the obnoxious comments coming from the guitarist and the bass player sitting behind me.

"Are we going to have to listen to the metronome for the whole two hours?"

"Tune it out. I need to practice 'Territorial Pissings' if we want to be ready for the concert tomorrow."

Two years ago, the four of us decided to start a Nirvana cover band. Over the past few months, we've started incorporating a few original compositions into our set list, but we've also come to accept that the

Kurt Cobain classics are what bring people to our concerts. Tomorrow night we're playing in a bar near Bastille. Alexandre, our singer, is the one who managed to find us a gig in Paris for the same weekend we were seeing Eagles of Death Metal. Two birds with one stone: part of the crowd on Friday, and up on stage on Saturday.

For over an hour, I try repeatedly to find the right rhythm, but I feel like I'll never get it. Behind me, Tiago is humming guitar chords to help me keep track of where I am in the song, but eventually I admit defeat and cut the tempo in half.

"Okay, guys, it's time to decide who's had the worst day, or, in other words, who drinks for free tonight!" declares Sylvain.

I turn off my metronome app and stash my sticks in the glove compartment.

"Who wants to go first?" Sylvain continues. "Come on now, no need to be shy!"

Alexandre glances over his shoulder before passing a truck going too slow for his taste, then dives into our usual game.

"Nothing special on my part. I spent the day wandering the streets hoping against hope that someone might actually spare a minute of their time listening to my fine rhetoric. Today I was stumping for a non-profit working to end world hunger. I hate to say it, but people don't give a *shit* about starving kids—especially not during their lunch break."

Alexandre is a street fund-raiser for several different charities. He knows his speeches by heart and exactly what to say to tug at the conscience of random strangers. He has to be overflowing with enthusiasm and cheer all day long, without batting an eyelid when he gets shot down by harried passersby.

"Today I got: 'Sorry, train to catch!' and 'That's great, but I already give money to the Humane Society; I can't fund every cause!' I had a guy point sadly at his headphones as if they were stuck on with glue, and I got an old lady who clutched her bag to her side, apparently convinced I was going to steal her coin purse. Oh, and the icing on the cake was the anorexic-looking chick in a mini skirt and high heels who said it was nice of me to ask, but she'd already had lunch. The nut job thought that my *End Hunger* campaign was about her!"

I burst into laughter while thinking to myself how glad I am not to have Alex's job.

"Okay, my turn," says Tiago.

He works for a moving company, and even though he's built like a linebacker, his days aren't exactly relaxing.

"Yesterday I emptied out my brother-in-law's one-bedroom apartment. He'd been renting it to some loser for years, a deadbeat who hadn't paid his rent in a year and a half. Then one day the guy up and left, without so much as a phone call; he just dropped his keys off at the rental agency. He left everything behind, as if he'd simply disappeared into thin air. And when we showed up at the apartment, it was the most disgusting thing we'd ever seen. The furniture was trashed and the walls were covered in mold, with some sort of green slime streaming down them onto the floor. There were cockroaches everywhere, and the floors were hidden under a layer of garbage. It was just plain nasty. And don't even get me started on the stench, which made us all sick for the two hours we spent emptying the place out . . ."

Alexandre makes a disgusted face, but Sylvain shouts, "Hey, wait! It doesn't count if it was yesterday! What'd you do *today*?"

"It was my day off," answers Tiago with a shrug.

"You're out, then, buddy!" exclaims Alexandre.

Tiago frowns but keeps quiet. He knows there's no point discussing the rules of the game since Sylvain makes them up as he goes—always to his advantage.

Sylvain clears his throat, preparing us for his tale. He works in an ad agency and always has the most unbelievable stories to share. I sometimes wonder if he makes a few of them up.

"Get this, guys. Today we were casting the new Yeastop commercial."

He inserts long pauses at the end of each sentence for maximum suspense. Occupational hazard, I guess.

"So *I* spent the whole morning watching beautiful girls deliver the line, 'Thanks to Yeastop, yeast isn't such a beast!'"

Alex, Tiago, and I shake our heads, unimpressed.

"Who thought up that shitty slogan?"

"Hey! No making fun. *I* came up with it!" Sylvain shouted angrily.

"I don't see what makes that a bad day," muses Tiago.

"Because you can't imagine what a turn-off it is when a gorgeous girl drops that line with a perfect smile. It's so awful that when one of them invited me to have lunch with her after the audition, I had to refuse because the sound of her voice made my crotch itch!"

"Yeah right," I muttered.

"Okay, wise guy, why don't you tell us about your day, Léopold. Then we'll see who gets to drink for free tonight!" countered Sylvain bitterly.

I can't help but sigh.

"Dude, it's like you always forget that I work on a pediatric oncology ward. Do you really want me to tell you about my day?"

My three bandmates indulge in a collective moan, then Sylvain adds, "All right, you win. But this is the last time! You're disqualified from all future rounds. We're tired of you making us sob with your sick-kid stories."

I look out the window without bothering to reply. Sylvain likes to joke, but despite his cool demeanor, I know that he couldn't do my job for even an hour. I can't help but think of Malo, whom I saw for the last time just before meeting up with the gang for this trip. Malo. Such a cute kid, only five years old and always so quick to smile. I've been taking care of him for almost a year, every time he comes to the hospital for chemotherapy. *Would you tell me a story, Léopold? Pretty please?* Every time I checked his stats or replaced a drip, I would invent a fairy tale—and the hero was always named Malo. But today his dad came to get him. He packed up all their things and took the *Cars* poster and family photos off the walls of the austere little room, then shook my hand a little more firmly than usual. Malo waved, almost shyly, as I watched him walk down the hall toward the exit, my throat tight. I felt so stupid. The kid was in total remission, and I had to be the only idiot who was sad about never seeing him again, never hearing his angelic little laugh as my stories got more and more unbelievable. It reminded me that no matter how things go in this job, I inevitably lose the children I can't help but get attached to.

"We'll be there in five minutes! No time to waste: we'll drop our stuff off at the hotel and head out right away. Do you have the tickets, Léo? What time does the opening act start?"

Alexandre's voice brings me back to reality, and I rummage through my inside jacket pocket to find the tickets I printed hastily this morning. For a split second, I'm afraid I've forgotten them—that would just make my day. Luckily, all four are there after all, and I sigh imperceptibly in relief.

6

MARGOT

The sullen expression on William's face as he puts his phone down is ominous.

"What is it?"

"The babysitter canceled. She can't watch Sacha tonight," he announces with a sigh.

"But I saw her downtown yesterday and she didn't say anything!"

I keep clearing the dining room table, fueled by anger.

"What's her excuse?"

"She said she was tired and had a hard week. She wanted to rest . . ."

"Are you kidding me, William? And you agreed and told her it was no big deal? That you *understood*?"

"Well, what was I supposed to say? It's not like I had any leverage. I can't *make* her come!"

"You could have told her that we bought these concert tickets months ago and that it's rude to cancel at the last minute."

"Fine, next time you handle the babysitter."

"No way will there be a next time for her. She's stood us up once, I'm not going to give her the chance to do it again."

Sacha is sitting in his playpen, cooing as he tosses all the toys he can reach onto the floor. At seven months, he's starting to realize that the world on the other side of the bars is much more interesting, and I know that pretty soon he'll throw a fit as soon as we try to put him down into it, among all the multicolored toys he already knows by heart.

William picks him up and sits down on the couch to read him a story.

But I refuse to give up. I hide out in Sacha's room and call William's mother—I'm desperate. As soon as she realizes what I'm asking, she eagerly jumps at my request to come over and take care of her beloved grandson.

I quickly lay Sacha's sleep sack in his crib, getting everything ready for bedtime. In the bathroom, I set out the diapers and his warm green pajamas where she'll be sure to see them. I want to make things as easy as possible for my mother-in-law . . .

When I return to the living room, William is trying to build a tower out of wooden blocks, but Sacha keeps sending it flying as soon as his father has three pastel-hued floors stacked up. My son bursts out laughing every time, and the exuberant expression on his face fills me with joy. I squat down to kiss his round little cheeks, and he leans in, clearly enjoying my affection.

"Your mother will be here in an hour."

William looks up with a frown.

"My mother? I thought you didn't trust her? That you wouldn't leave her alone with Sacha until he's an adult?"

"Let's just say I've decided to give her a chance."

My husband calls my bluff.

"*Or* we could say that you really don't want to give up your night out!" he replies teasingly.

William knows me like the back of his hand. I've been looking forward to tonight for weeks, to a night out, just the two of us . . .

I have to admit that when I decided to take six extra months off at the end of my three-month maternity leave, I overestimated my ability to spend twenty-four hours a day with my baby. I had imagined only the good parts, like how much I would enjoy watching my son grow and develop without missing a single second. Plus, William and I had done the math: given my pittance of a salary working as a medical secretary in a dentist's office and the exorbitant price of childcare in Villejuif, we wouldn't lose much money if I stayed home. And it would be easier on Sacha, who wouldn't have to deal with long days away from home at the age of three months. It was an easy choice to make. My love for my son is unconditional and overwhelming—to the point of getting up several times a night to make sure he's still breathing, along with the pure pleasure of watching him sleep peacefully—but now that fall is here, I must admit I'm looking forward to going back to work, to having a social life, to freely coming and going as I please.

"Should we give him his bath before my mom gets here?"

William's voice brings me back to reality, and I head to the bathroom to run the water.

I play with Sacha in his tub while my husband changes out of his suit and tie and into black jeans and a hoodie. I watch as my son splashes energetically, then wonders how his face got all wet, and I realize how impossible it is for me to imagine life without him. Of course I remember perfectly how things were before, before our life was filled with his laughter and shrieking. I know that the world used to exist without Sacha, but that time seems so far away now, as if I'd spent the first thirty-one years of my life simply waiting for him to come along.

My mother-in-law shows up at seven thirty with a big book tucked under her arm. *The Future Is in Your Palm.* A promising title . . .

"I'm going to practice on Sacha! Apparently our futures are written in the palms of our hands!" she declares enthusiastically.

I'm tempted to explain that since he's barely seven months old, I doubt his lines are particularly legible or definitive, but I hold my tongue. After all, William's mother is doing us a favor tonight. Without her, I'd have to forget about Eagles of Death Metal.

"That's great, Patricia! Then you can see if your predictions match the tarot-card reading and the full horoscope you did for him," I say, trying hard to remove all traces of skepticism and mockery from my voice.

It must work, because my mother-in-law nods vigorously. "Exactly!" I button my coat as she continues, "And let's not forget that this little cutie is here in part thanks to me!"

I must have heard this a couple dozen times since Sacha was born. Patricia will never forget that if it weren't for her, William and I might never have met, though there's nothing particularly romantic about the story. She sent her son to the other side of town to find her some star anise at an organic grocery store in my neighborhood, and he entered the place just as I walked in to stock up on tea. The short version is that one thing then led to another, and now we have Sacha.

So for the rest of my life, I'll have to listen to my mother-in-law continually remind us of how she brought us together, and how neither of us would ever have found love without her remarkable talents as a matchmaker . . .

Once we're in the elevator, William rifles through his wallet and realizes he doesn't have any cash.

"Do you have any?"

"You know I never have cash. I even use a card when I buy a baguette."

"We'll have to run back upstairs, then. I'm sure the T-shirt stand won't take cards. They never do . . ."

When we finally get to the parking garage, William climbs into the driver's side of our old Clio while I think back to make sure I've explained everything my mother-in-law needs to do. The bottle: seven ounces, plus two scoops of cereal. The diaper and diaper cream. The nightlight in his room and the baby monitor. The Camilia for his tender teething gums, even though Patricia has more faith in her tarot cards than in homeopathic remedies. The Tylenol and the thermometer left out in the bathroom where she can see them, just in case.

"The car won't start!"

William keeps turning the key in the ignition, but not a sound troubles the silence that reigns in the dark garage. I let out a weary sigh.

"Are we cursed or what? I'm starting to think Sacha worked some sort of black magic to keep us from going out without him!"

My husband glances at his watch: 7:54 p.m.

"If we hurry, we can make it by Metro."

I grab my purse and get out of the car. William is already a few yards ahead of me. I hurry to catch up with him. Once we reach the street, he takes my hand and we run for the station, usually a fifteen-minute walk away.

"Come on! Nothing's going to keep us from having our night out!"

7

DAPHNÉ

Today, like every weekday, is a race against the clock, a fight to keep time from slipping through my fingers. I'm the White Rabbit from *Alice in Wonderland*. I'm late, I'm late, I'm late. And I don't need a watch to know it. I have to be at the school by six fifteen to get Charline, but I'll never make it. Best-case scenario, if I run as fast as I can and arrive at the gates covered in sweat, I'll still be ten minutes late. As is the case almost every evening, I'll be the last parent to pick up her child, and the school principal will smirk, letting me know exactly how she feels about me, the Bad Mother Who's Always Late: *Thank goodness other parents aren't like you, or we'd never be able to close the school gates . . .* When I walk past her again on my way out with Charline, she'll ask mockingly, *Do you realize how hard it is to teach children to respect principles that their parents don't heed?* I'll want to slap her and offer to let her spend a day doing my job as a supermarket cashier while I do hers, but instead I'll keep my head down like a scolded child, ashamed to be humiliated like that in front of my daughter.

But luck is on my side for once, because when I get to school, the other parents are waiting impatiently in front of the closed gate. I check the time on my phone. There's no mistake; I'm exactly ten minutes late. At the far end of the playground, I see a figure running toward the school entrance. Keys in hand, the principal, Mrs. Coullet, hurries toward us, out of breath.

"I'm so sorry. I had to take care of something and it kept me from getting here on time . . ."

The parents gripe as they wait for their children to come out. I make eye contact with the woman who so enjoys belittling me and offer a dazzling smile.

"Don't worry about it," I say magnanimously. "Everyone gets delayed sometimes!"

Charline finally comes through the gate and throws herself into my arms, all wrapped up in her pink puffer coat, which she absolutely had to put on this morning despite the fact that it's nowhere near cold enough for it.

"Did you have a good day, sweetie?"

"Yes! Louise invited me to her birthday party Saturday afternoon, so we need to buy her a present . . ."

"Fine, we'll do that Saturday morning."

I go through the list of everything else we have to do Saturday and wonder how I'm going to fit this into our already jam-packed schedule.

"Could we go now instead, Mommy? We could stop at the mall on the way home?"

I sigh as I think of the dinner to be made, homework to be done, and things to be readied for tomorrow, but when I see the pleading look on my daughter's face, I can't help but give in.

"Well, I guess that'll be one less thing to do Saturday morning . . ."

It's after seven when Charline and I finally get home. For a second, I let myself hope that it occurred to Julien to make dinner, but the apartment is dark and I realize he isn't even home from work. Looks I'll be spending yet another evening rushing to get everything done.

"I'm going to see what's in the freezer for dinner. While I'm doing that, go get cleaned up and put on your pajamas, okay? And hurry up!"

I turn on the lights in the living room while simultaneously taking off my ankle boots, almost jumping out of my skin when I hear "Surprise!" shouted in chorus by the fifteen people who've been hiding quietly until now.

My husband, Julien, comes over to kiss me and whispers, "Happy birthday!" in my ear, before moving over to let our guests hug me and wish me well. Charline is laughing.

"Were you in on this?"

"Of course! Why else would I have begged you to go buy Louise's present tonight?"

I tousle her hair, surprised that my eight-year-old chatterbox managed to keep such a big secret. My parents are preparing hors d'oeuvres in the kitchen. My sister, some longtime girlfriends, a few coworkers, and a couple with a daughter the same age as Charline are gathered in the living room.

"But you know my birthday's not until tomorrow, right?"

"You're working tomorrow night and Saturday night, so I had to move the party up a bit! And celebrating early isn't so bad. This way, you didn't suspect a thing . . ."

My husband wraps his arms around my shoulders, clearly pleased with his surprise. It's true that I'll be at the Bataclan tomorrow and Saturday. In September, my boss at the store cut my hours, so I had to find something else to make ends meet. So now I spend two nights a week working the coat check at the concert hall instead of standing behind a cash register. The good part is that the people there are usually nicer than the customers at the store—most likely because they've just spent a fun evening out instead of a couple of hours doing their grocery shopping.

◆ ◆ ◆

We have a lovely evening. Everyone goes out of their way to make sure I'm having fun, and for once I feel relaxed—even if in a far corner of my mind, I'm still thinking about everything I have to do before going to bed.

When it's time for cake and presents, Julien brings in a huge Paris-Brest—my favorite dessert—with praline pastry cream overflowing down the sides. A four and a zero sparkle atop it in the muted light of the living room. I close my eyes and blow as hard as I can. Charline claps delightedly.

"Did you remember to make a wish, Mommy?"

"Of course, pumpkin, but wishes are secret!"

Actually, I didn't think to wish for anything at all. I was too preoccupied, trying to remember to call the ophthalmologist in the morning to make an appointment for my daughter. I've been putting it off for two weeks, and now I'm sure there won't be any slots available before spring . . .

I do my best to put my worries aside and concentrate on the gifts to be opened. My parents give me a bottle of wine, a 1975 Château Margaux that my father must have been carefully hiding in his cellar for my fortieth birthday for years. I'll open it the next time they come over for dinner. Julien hands me a small black velvet box. I open it to find a delicate amethyst ring. I look at him affectionately, touched that he remembered how I had marveled at the beautiful piece of jewelry in the window of a downtown boutique. My sister had put together a box with exactly forty different bottles of nail polish. She knows how much I love my nails to match my outfits, and now I've got every color under the sun! My friends and coworkers have all pooled their money to buy me a weekend in Venice in February. I'm sure Julien must have helped them with their choice, since he knows I've always wanted to see Carnival there . . .

The last present is from Charline, who's biting her nails anxiously as she waits for me to open it. I rip off the paper and pull out a green beaded necklace with three strands.

"I made it myself," she hastens to add.

"It's beautiful, honey!"

I fasten it around my neck and all the guests ooh and aah enthusiastically.

The party is still in full force when I put Charline to bed. She hugs me tight.

"Do you really like your present?" she asks. "I chose four shades of green to make it even prettier . . ."

"Or course I do, sweetie. I'll tell you a secret: I think it's my favorite present of all, because you made it yourself! The time you spent working on it is priceless."

Reassured, Charline closes her eyes and curls herself into a ball on her side. I get up and quietly close the door to her room, thinking to myself just how priceless time really is. And how I have *got* to start a load of laundry before the hamper overflows.

8

Théo

"First one upstairs wins!"

Before I've even finished my sentence, I'm rushing up the stairs two by two.

"I'm taking the elevator, Théo! You've already lost!" Dad yells from behind me.

My father's kidding himself if he thinks he can win that easily. I know I'll make it to the sixth floor before him—piece of cake. I pause on every landing and frantically push the elevator button, so he'll be slowed down by stopping at every floor. What a dummy for not thinking of that before he got in!

By the time I've reached the fourth floor, I don't even bother running anymore. I know I've won, so there's no point in hurrying. Dad will be even more annoyed when he sees me waiting calmly in front of the door to the apartment, bored and tapping my Flik Flak watch. But a surprise is waiting for me on the welcome mat where I always carefully wipe my shoes so Dad doesn't get cranky—he's kind of a neat freak, even though he won't admit it. Mom is already there to pick me up, and from the look on her face, we must be late.

Thanks to her, my stunning victory goes unnoticed, because when the elevator bell dings and my father dashes out (he must really still think he can win), he stops short at the sight of my mother tapping her foot. I can tell there's going to be a shouting match, so I quickly grab the keys from his hand and go inside to stuff my things into my backpack. The faster I'm ready, the less shrieky Mom's voice will get. I've become an expert over the years.

The front door is half open, so I can hear my parents' discussion. They're talking about me, as usual—I'm the only thing they have to talk about since the divorce.

"I'll pick him up from school next Friday. I'm taking him to a concert in Paris that night, and to the science museum on Saturday."

"A concert?"

Here we go, Mom's just getting started. He should have seen it coming.

"Yes, a rock concert! It'll be his first, and he'll remember it for the rest of his life!"

"Don't you think he's a bit too young for that? He's only ten, and you already want to expose him to deafening music? Plus, he could get smothered by the crowd in a place like that . . ."

I have no trouble imagining Mom shaking her head, hands on her hips. And Dad still doesn't realize what he's gotten himself into. He still thinks he can sweet-talk her, calm her down with a snap of his fingers.

"How exactly are you planning to get to Paris?"

Dad's clearly thought it all out. I can hear the pride in his voice.

"We'll take the train, of course! It's only two hours from Lyon. And Théo's been begging me to take him to Paris for months. Doesn't seem like too much to ask."

"Well, it's not supposed to be your weekend . . ."

Mom's grumbling more quietly now, and I think it's in the bag. If Dad can just keep from saying something stupid at the last minute, she'll let us go. I cross my fingers as hard as I can behind my back and underneath my striped sweater, to help my dad get through it. I hear him persuading my mother, promising her that he'll be careful, reminding her that I'm growing up (and he's right, I'm not a baby anymore).

"Okay," she finally whispers, and I jump for joy.

They turn toward me, surprised that I've been eavesdropping. They still have a lot to learn about children.

Mom asks me if I really want to go to the concert and I tell her yes, that it's going to be awesome and that I'm looking forward to bragging about it at school the following Monday. She doesn't seem totally convinced, but she admits defeat.

Dad looks triumphant as he says, "See you Friday, buddy!" and hands me my backpack, which I dropped on the floor in all the excitement.

Once we're out on the street, Mom stops pouting and offers to take me shopping for a new pair of sneakers.

"Thanks, Mom, but mine are still in good shape. And it's cooler for them to look used anyway."

She won't give up easily, though, so she asks if the weekend after the concert I'd like to go to the movies.

"I dunno, I don't think there's anything good showing right now . . ."

"We could go bowling, then?"

I shake my head. Bowling isn't really my thing.

"Or you could invite some friends over? That'd be nice, wouldn't it?"

She looks desperate and I feel sorry for her.

"You know, Mom, just because Dad's taking me to Paris doesn't mean you have to try and one-up him."

She blushes and mumbles that that's not what she's trying to do, that she doesn't understand why she can't simply do something nice for her son anymore.

"Don't worry, Mom. I love both of you the same. There's no need for competition!"

I can tell she's surprised that at the age of ten I already understand what they're up to, but I don't want her to be sad or think that Dad has better ideas. Even if it is kinda true. I mean, a rock concert, that's so cool! I can't imagine what she could suggest that would be better—which says a lot . . .

Mom suddenly perks up. I can tell because she stands up tall again and walks straight ahead.

"In that case, when we get home we'll go over your homework for next week. Don't you have a presentation on the human body to do?"

I sigh heavily. Mom is a real pro, she managed to fool me again. For all I know, she was never even really planning to take me shopping for new shoes!

When we get home, Olivier is working in the garage. It looks like he's trying to fix up Mom's old desk. She's been asking him to sand and varnish it for months.

"So, Théo, did you have a good weekend with your dad?"

I stick out my chest, ready to make him green with envy.

"Yeah, and guess what? Next weekend he's taking me to a rock concert!"

"You're a lucky kid! Wanna give me a hand redoing this desk?"

"No, thanks. I'd rather go finish my homework."

I head up without another word, but notice the wounded look on my stepfather's face out of the corner of my eye. I know he's disappointed and wishes we spent more time together, especially since my mom is always afraid I'll think he's trying to take Dad's place. I don't mind Olivier, though. He's a nice guy. It's just that I don't want Mom to have it too easy. It's nice when she spoils me and fawns over me . . . so sometimes I'm hard on him.

◆ ◆ ◆

I sit in the big rocking chair in my room and get out the two tickets Dad agreed to let me keep till the concert.

"Eagles of Death Metal." The letters are printed in all caps. I slowly run my finger over the black ink. My first concert ticket. I think about how I'll pin it to my wall as soon as I get back from Paris.

I put the CD Dad got me into my little stereo and bob my head to the beat, wishing my hair were a little longer so I'd look more legit. The lyrics are all in English, which sounds like gibberish to me, but that doesn't keep me from excitedly humming the few syllables I think I recognize.

In my spiral datebook, I circle Friday, November 13, with a thick red marker, then stick out my tongue in concentration as I decorate the page with a dozen or so music notes.

9

LUCAS

Even now, after several years together, Anouk can still surprise me. I have no idea how she does it.

"How did you manage to get the tickets? It's been sold out forever!"

She looks at me, eyebrow cocked mischieviously, clearly pleased with herself.

"I bought them this summer. It's this thing called *planning ahead*, smarty-pants."

It's true that foresight is hardly my strong suit. I can't even count the number of awesome concerts I've missed because I only realized the tickets were on sale once they were already sold out.

"So what's the occasion?"

Anouk lets out a long sigh, and I start running through things in my mind to figure out why.

"What do you think?"

Uh-oh. Looks like I've put my foot in my mouth. It's not my birthday, and it's obviously not hers, so it doesn't take me too long to realize it's our anniversary. Our fifth anniversary. Nice round numbers like that deserve a little celebration—when you're not an idiot like me.

"I left your present at home. I didn't think we'd exchange gifts here . . ."

I doubt I've fooled her, and even if I have, it won't take her long to realize I don't really have anything for her when we get back to our apartment. I'll have to come up with something good! Lucky for me, she chooses not to say anything, clearly not wanting to ruin the moment.

"Do you want to go together?"

"Obviously! I didn't give you two tickets so you could take someone else," she exclaims teasingly.

"Are you sure you'll be okay?"

I have to ask because I know that Anouk is a bit claustrophobic, and she's usually not crazy about being squished in the middle of a dense, wildly dancing crowd. For example, in the hospital where she works as an apprentice midwife, she knows exactly how many steps it takes to get from her basement office to the door leading outside. I'm exaggerating a little, of course, but I'm not too far off.

She shakes her head, annoyed.

"I'm not made of glass, you know. Can't you just say you're excited for us to go to the concert together? You've been making me listen to *Zipper Down* on repeat for over a month now. I know some of their songs by heart!"

Anouk's best friend, Jessica, agrees with a series of overly enthusiastic nods.

"She's right, Lucas. Plus, we'll be there too! It'll be fun for all four of us to have a night out."

Anouk lights a cigarette and takes a quick puff—a sure sign of irritation. The waiter finally brings our drinks, and we wait until he leaves to trade glasses so that each of has what we actually ordered.

I glance toward Djibril, who's staying out of it, his eyes focused on the screwdriver in his glass. He's learned that there's no point trying to argue with women.

After blowing a few perfect, sexy smoke rings, Anouk reminds me of how much she adores "I Love You All the Time" and that she's eager to hear it "for real." I want to reply that it's the tamest song on the entire album, and hardly representative of what an Eagles of Death Metal concert will be like, but Djibril kicks me under the table and I stop myself.

"It'll be great, then! Thanks, honey."

I kiss Anouk while discreetly massaging my shin and thinking about the amazing gift I now have to find if I want to get off the hook for forgetting our anniversary in the first place.

It's getting late when it starts to rain, a light sprinkle that holds the promise of an imminent downpour. Like all the other customers sitting on the terrace, we grab our glasses and hurry inside. Raindrops stream down Anouk's face as she pulls her thick hair into a ponytail. I think about kissing her under the stormy sky—the same color as her eyes. She would find that incredibly romantic; she loves romantic comedies, and happy endings, and Hugh Grant. You can't get more romantic than kissing in the rain. But I don't like to get wet—I hate the feeling of rain running down my neck onto my back and of wet jeans sticking to my thighs. Worst of all is not being able to see because of the drops covering my glasses. Hugh Grant doesn't ever seem to have such problems. I'm sure an entire army of hair dryers rolls up as soon as his rain scenes have been shot, but Anouk doesn't know that. She prefers to think that Hollywood is real life, and that the best way to make up after a fight is to storm out of the apartment and slam the door, hoping that I'll run after her throwing rose petals at her feet. But I'm not sure she even expects me to do things like that anymore, since I've always stayed true to myself—I've never been a very sentimental kind of guy.

I grab my beer and her gin fizz and we head quickly into the bar. As soon as I've set our drinks down on the first free table, I grab her arm and pull her in close for a kiss. A long, passionate kiss. I brush aside a strand of hair from her eyes and feel her wet lips on mine. We forget where we are for a second.

"Get a room!" Jessica says with a smirk.

Anouk and I pretend not to hear—proof that there's no need to get drenched in the rain for a kiss to be romantic.

We met on the Internet our first year of college, on a dating site that was so lame I doubt it even exists anymore. A buddy from school signed me up one night after we'd had way too much to drink. Anouk sent me a message a week later, when I had already totally forgotten about it. I wrote back, just to see. She must have had the same idea. We exchanged e-mails for a long while—she wasn't in a hurry to meet. Her romantic side yet again, I assume. An epistolary romance was very Richard Gere (because, obviously, Hugh Grant isn't her only reference).

Two months later, we finally made plans to meet in front of the Créteil train station—and I forgot to show up. The date totally slipped my mind until I got a text message asking if something had come up. Epic fail. I ran as fast as I could to the train station, almost getting run over about a dozen times on the way. When I saw a woman waiting all alone out front, I knew right away it was Anouk. She was exactly how I'd imagined her. Only better. I'm not sure she thought the same thing about me as I stood in front of her, all sweaty, with giant pit stains on my shirt. But she pretended not to notice and, after listening to my excuses with a dubious look on her face, she decided to give me a chance. Good thing too, because man, would it have sucked if we hadn't made it past the first date.

As we're heading home arm in arm at one in the morning, a bit tipsy, I finally admit I don't have a present waiting for her at home.

"No kidding," she replies sarcastically, with a slight slur.

"Hey, how about a ticket to an awesome concert next week?"

She laughs. "Do not tell me you're trying to regift me half of the present I just gave you."

I look sheepishly down at my feet.

"Just take me out to dinner this week, jeez . . ."

I sigh in relief, thinking how lucky I am to have such an accommodating girlfriend.

"A fancy restaurant, though, okay?"

I nod and a brilliant idea pops into my head.

"You got it. Candles and white tablecloths."

Anouk smiles, and I'm surprised not to hear a sappy violin melody playing in the background—the perfect accompaniment to this scene straight out of a great silver-screen love story.

10

ROMANE

If my calculations are correct, and the man behind the counter at the post office is at all trustworthy, my letter should have arrived in my little sister Adèle's mailbox this morning. Now all I have to do is work up the courage to call her. It's after eleven; she must be up by now.

She answers on the first ring, which is hardly surprising given she's never far from her smartphone. The hello on the other end of the line sounds a bit sleepy. I hope I haven't woken her up—she's never in a good mood first thing in the morning.

"I was just calling to see how you're doing. It's been a while since we've talked . . ."

"I didn't know my life interested you."

I was expecting a difficult conversation, and, true to form, it doesn't look like Adèle's inclined to make things easy for me. At twenty-three, she hasn't yet learned the meaning of the word *compromise*, or that everything in life isn't always black and white . . .

"Look, things haven't been good between us for a while, and I was thinking we could bury the hatchet once and for all."

Adèle doesn't answer; she just waits. I hear the muffled sound of a lighter and her first puff of a cigarette as she stays silent.

"How are things in Dijon? Mom and Dad good?"

"Great."

"Are you getting settled in your apartment?"

"There are still a bunch of boxes to unpack, but it's starting to come together."

She makes zero effort to hold up her side of the conversation or raise new topics. I'm starting to think maybe it wasn't such a good idea to call her after all.

"And . . . your job?"

"Really good. We're already all booked up for December with shows in daycares and schools. The company is starting to make a name for itself around the city."

After two years of law school, Adèle suddenly decided to become a stage actor. She totally overhauled her plans for the future, against the advice of everyone around her. Our parents dug in their heels, convinced that she'd only changed course because of the boy she was dating at the time, a kind of bougie Rasta guy who spent his days trying to walk across an elastic band stretched between two trees. But my little sister held her ground and got a degree in theater before joining a small troupe whose name always escapes me.

"That's great! I'm really glad that your career path is working out—"

"'Career path?' Do you hear yourself, Romane? It's like you don't know how to talk normally anymore. All that comes out of your mouth is uptight administrative jargon! I'm an actress and proud of it, even if it's not the kind of career everybody dreams of."

"Why do you always have to be so defensive? When I say I'm happy for you, that's what I mean . . ."

"Oh really? You weren't here to support me when our parents did everything possible to make me stay in law school! You weren't here to tell them that I could choose my own path, that it didn't have to include what they call a 'conventional' profession. You didn't defend me when Dad said that only losers and nut jobs want to be actors!"

It's true that I didn't immediately side with Adèle three years ago when she decided to pursue acting. I thought it was just another one of her whims, one that she'd get over in a couple of weeks and that she'd regret when she realized she'd lost a year of school for nothing. The theater . . . I never would have thought anyone could make a living at it, or that anyone would ever want to live with that kind of insecurity, not knowing what tomorrow holds. So, no, I didn't back her up, even though I knew quite well that no matter what our parents said, my sister would do whatever she wanted.

Now all I want is to make up with her, but I'm not sure I can if she won't meet me halfway.

"I'm sorry I wasn't openly on your side. But I did lend you money when you needed it. And you didn't even have to ask . . ."

On the other end of the line, I hear Adèle quietly exhaling the smoke from her cigarette.

"That's true."

"I was ending things with Gaëtan at the time, and I didn't have anyone to help me out either."

She doesn't answer, and I don't know if it's because she's thinking about what I've just said, or because she's simmering and about to explode—she often says I always make everything about me.

"You know, just because I'm six years older doesn't mean it should always be my responsibility to smooth things over with Mom and Dad, and console you when you're feeling down. I wouldn't mind having a more supportive sister when things are tough . . ."

I keep talking even though I'm convinced she's going to hang up on me. Strangely, that doesn't happen.

"Okay, so what do you suggest?" she asks, as the anger disappears from her voice and she lowers her guard.

"Well, I was thinking we could be a little more invested in each other's lives in the future. And communicate before things deteriorate between us."

"We should call each other more often too," adds Adèle.

"Actually, we should *see* each other more often," I correct her. I'm delighted she's given me the opportunity to bring up what I've been wanting to talk about since the beginning of our conversation.

"Are you planning to come down to Dijon soon?" she asks, surprised.

She knows I love my life in Paris and that I rarely spend a weekend in the city I grew up in. Between my job at the Ministry of Culture, the conferences and other events I'm responsible for (which always take place on Saturdays), and the cooking classes I give in my little apartment on Sundays to share my passion for food, my calendar is pretty full. My mother often chides me about it when I call.

"Well, I was actually thinking you might like to come to Paris for a weekend—"

Adèle's voice trills with joy. I have no trouble imagining the delighted expression on her face.

"Obviously! I'd love to!"

"In that case, I think you'd better go check your mail."

"What?"

"Make your way down the eight flights of stairs to your mailbox and then call me back, okay?"

Adèle hangs up, confused. I'm already smiling as I wait for her reaction.

Less than five minutes later—she must have run all the way down the stairs and then back up again—my phone rings, and a hysterical voice only narrowly misses bursting my eardrums.

"How'd you know?"

"Just because we haven't been on the best of terms doesn't mean I forgot your taste in music . . ."

"Eagles of Death Metal next month, Romane! This is so awesome!"

I'm the one who introduced her to the band a few years back, before they became popular in France.

"And you bought my train tickets too?"

"Yep, it's an all-inclusive package. That way, the only thing you have to worry about is your outfit . . ."

I know that Adèle isn't exactly rolling in it, even if she is able to make ends meet from her job with the troupe. And I didn't want money to be an obstacle to our reconciliatory weekend.

"I already know what I'm going to wear! I'm not the kind of girl who spends hours in front of her closet!"

I'm not sure if that's a barb meant for me, since I *am* the kind of person who spends hours in front of her wardrobe hesitating between two almost-identical dresses.

"You can wear the boots I bought you for Christmas last year! I've never seen you wear them, and this is the perfect occasion!"

I decide not to tell Adèle that the reason I've never worn the red cowboy boots is because she got them in a seven and I wear an eight.

Oh well, I'll scrunch up my toes for one night. I can survive a few hours of torture to make her happy.

II

DURING

1

ABIGAËLLE

When the loud bell I've been waiting for finally interrupts my history teacher's soporific monologue, I'm the first student to grab my backpack and hurry to the restroom on the ground floor. It's 6:35 p.m. I'm meeting Clara in exactly fifty-five minutes. In other words, no time to lose.

I get out my makeup bag and use my eyeliner and some charcoal-gray eyeshadow to create a smoky-eye look. A touch of mascara, and I'm off.

"I almost had to wait for you," mumbles Clara.

She's leaning against the stairs to the Metro station, rolling one of her long blonde dreads between her hands as if trying to light a fire.

"I'm not even five minutes late! Quit whining!"

With an impish grin, I place my leg next to hers. We have on the same turquoise tights, awesome! As we walk toward the Bataclan in step, Clara tells me about her afternoon. She seems to be on a mission to prove to me that her teachers are even more boring than mine.

My phone rings from inside my leather jacket, interrupting my friend. The screen reads "Mom," obviously. I wait patiently for my Muse ringtone to quiet—I don't want my mom to think that I'm deliberately refusing her call. Clara gives me a questioning glance.

"What did you end up telling her?"

"Nothing. I got out of school at six thirty and should have been home half an hour later. I guess since I'm now over half an hour late, she's worried and annoyed, pacing the halls at home by herself. I bet she's recruiting my dad as back-up and he'll be calling in the next twenty seconds."

As if to confirm my suspicions, Matthew Bellamy's voice starts singing "Mercy" again, loudly.

"Is that him?" Clara asks doubtfully.

"No. My mistake. It's my mom again. Just in case I didn't hear it the first time."

I wait for my voicemail to pick up, then silence my phone so I'll be left in peace.

"Maybe you should tell her we're at the concert so she doesn't worry too much?" suggests my best friend with a frown.

"No, no point. I'm sure she'll get to the bottom of my disappearance on her own after a while."

Clara shrugs without a word. I know exactly what she's thinking: that it's not cool to let my parents worry, that I could at least send them a text. But really, I feel like maybe it's a good thing if my mom worries about me a bit. Maybe that way, when I get home tonight, she'll have a little perspective. She'll be so relieved that nothing's happened to me, that I only defied her.

We're finally at the concert hall. I'm scanning the place so intently to find Ilan that I barely notice as the bouncer stamps my hand. The opening band is already playing as I look around the dark venue, ignoring Clara's smirk.

"Help me find him instead of laughing like a jerk."

"Do you see a crown?" she asks as if she's really invested. She's holding her right hand over her eyes and studying the crowd as people move toward the stage.

"What crown?"

"You know, Prince Charming always wears a crown, doesn't he?"

"Very funny. I'm gonna head up to the balcony to get a better view."

Clara follows me, chuckling heartily at her own joke. At the T-shirt stand, I notice a woman wearing red cowboy boots. I nudge my friend.

"Do you see her boots? They're awesome! Wait, I'm going to take a quick picture so I can put them on my Christmas list."

I don't even try to be discreet as I snap the picture of the brunette, because she's completely focused on the selection of Eagles of Death Metal T-shirts. With a simple click, the cowboy boots are in my phone's memory. Before stashing it in my pocket, I notice I have two missed calls and a text message. Guess my mom's not all that worried after all.

We manage to make our way to the balcony, which is already pretty full, and I search for Ilan in the crowd below, in vain. Either he's not here yet, or I'm a terrible spotter. I drag Clara back down to the pit with me.

"Let's go right up to the stage. Ilan's a serious fan; I bet he'll want to be as close to the band as possible."

We shove past a few people on our way, constantly saying, "Sorry, our friends are in the front row. We just want to get to them!" and offering insincere smiles. When we finally make it to the stage, I freeze. There's Ilan! To our left, with his group of friends whose names I don't know. There are only a few people between us.

I watch his face, gracefully lit by the spotlights from the stage, then do my best to wipe the stupid grin off mine before nodding to Clara, who follows my gaze.

"I guess we'll be staying here?"

I giggle softly and feel myself blush. I try to focus on the singer as she jumps around energetically, finishing her last song, but my mind is elsewhere. Applause and enthusiastic whistling sound all around me, and I automatically start clapping in rhythm with the rest of the audience. When the duo leaves the stage and the crowd begins to quiet, Clara takes advantage of the relative calm to tell me yet again how cute her Spanish teacher is. I'm sure a simple roll of his tongue is enough for her to immediately melt at her desk and sigh in pleasure. Clara is always all in when she's crushing, especially when it's never going to happen: the more impossible the guy, the more she fantasizes about him. Last year, she was head over heels in love with the one and only gay guy in her class. She was almost convinced she could get him to change teams! I open my mouth to tell her she'd be better off forgetting her Juanes look-alike, but the band comes on stage and cuts me off with an explosion of drums and guitar. The crowd starts moving to the beat, and Clara and I do the same. I briefly close my eyes and let myself be carried away by Jesse Hughes's nasally voice. We'll have plenty of time to edge ourselves to the left during the concert. The important thing is not to lose sight of my target.

After several songs spent glancing insistently at Ilan, our eyes finally meet. He pauses for a second, probably sifting through his memories to figure out who I am. It's true that we've only spoken a few times at parties, and I know I'm not exactly unforgettable, despite all my efforts to seem eccentric. He finally nods and smiles briefly. I wave, a surprised look on my face—*what a coincidence, running into each other at this concert!* He turns back toward the stage and starts moshing with his friends again. I take advantage of his lapse in attention to crab walk to the left. Clara follows, clinging to me.

As I start moving in cadence with the drums again, a blaring, popping sound suddenly makes me jump. It's like fireworks have just gone off in the concert hall, and when I say fireworks, I mean the big finale.

I'm thinking how awesome this concert is when I notice the look on the singer's face. Stunned. Disbelieving. Almost frightened.

That's when we all turn around in unison. I see flashes of orange light and hear staccato bursts getting louder and louder. I'm petrified. The seconds stretch on forever. The lights come back on and I squint, blinded. I freeze, unable to understand what's going on. People are shoving violently. I hear screaming and feel the overwhelming sense of panic in the room. I have to move, to run, but I can't budge. Only a yard away, I see a girl my age crumple to the floor. She's so close I can tell she's wearing purple mascara and that it's got clumps in it. Her strangely vacant green eyes meet mine, and in that fraction of a second, I understand.

I turn and run toward the stage as fast as I can, head lowered. I'm a terrible athlete, but I climb over the security gate without a second thought, then over the people who've chosen to lie down or squat. There's only instinct now, the instinct of a hunted animal. I hear continuous bursts of gunfire exploding everywhere, exploding in my head, hissing past as bodies drop all around me. As I use my arms to climb up onto the stage, I suddenly feel a shooting pain in my back, then another in my thigh. Like a whip lashing my skin, it sends me to the floor. I stumble and land flat on my stomach. Someone walks on my arm, trampling me without stopping. All I can see are sneakers with blue-and-white stripes hurrying away.

Then, all of a sudden, it goes silent. The gunfire stops, leaving only the screaming, the crying, and the noise of rushing feet. I exhale quietly and start crawling, lifting my head as little as possible. I can't feel my left leg anymore; it's like it's fallen asleep. The shots start up again and I keep moving, slowly, until I manage to get behind a bunch of amps that make up a kind of rampart. Just like my fort, when I used to stack books to make a castle and Clara would play the evil witch. Where is she anyway?

To my right, I see dozens of people running to hide. Meanwhile, here I am, alone on the stage, unable to stand. I want to call out to them, ask them to help me, not to leave me, to scream so they come back—they can't just abandon me here—but no sound leaves my mouth. I huddle into the fetal position to make myself as small as possible, to disappear, when I notice something wet between my legs. Shit, have I peed myself? I can't help but think how embarrassing this is and hope that I won't run into Ilan now, even though some part of me knows that's the least of my problems. I run my fingers over my tights and feel a warm, sticky liquid dripping onto the ground. When I see the color of my hand, I clench my jaw to keep from screaming. Shh, don't make any noise, don't attract attention, play dead. A wave of terror rushes up my throat, but I keep my mouth shut, like when Clara mimes *zip it* to tell me to keep a secret. My lips are sealed; you can count on me. But that doesn't keep the questions from popping into my head relentlessly, without any answers. Am I bleeding to death? Am I going to die here, from a bullet to the leg? If I put pressure on it, will it help? If I had paid more attention in biology, would I know what to do? If I stay still and breathe as little as possible, will I bleed less?

I notice that the waves of gunfire have tapered off, replaced by single shots. Is that a good thing or not? Who are these guys? What do they want with us? What have we done to them? What have *I* done to them? Why are they taking it out on us like this for no apparent reason?

Little by little everyone around me quiets down. The screams become rare and scattered, and when one does break the heavy silence, I shake in terror. I hate that I can hear myself trembling, that I can hear my pulse buzzing in my ears. Every sign of life heightens the risk of death. I think of my dad's freediving techniques: save oxygen, slow your heartbeat, hold your breath, slow your mind, come back into the light.

I put as much pressure as possible on my upper thigh, and, before I black out, I wonder if Clara's okay, if she was able to get out of here, if she escaped *without me*, if these amps can really protect me from anything, if it's not too late for me to come back to the surface.

2

PHILIPPE

When Pascal unzips his jacket and pulls out a box of earplugs, then carefully opens it, I realize how much he's aged in the past few months. I can't help but sneak a quick look around us to make sure no one's noticed this heretical act, but people are too busy making their way toward the stage to pay attention to my friend's earplugs. We already stand out thanks to his camel cowboy hat, but this takes the cake. I'm just glad to see Pascal smiling, forgetting his day-to-day problems, so I keep my mouth shut.

He enthusiastically holds out the transparent little box, home to three pairs of neon plugs. As I shake my head to let him know I'll go without, two girls rush by and shove us in their hurry to reach the front row. One of them, whose blonde dreads are disproportionately long and voluminous given her tiny face, turns around to mutter an insincere sorry, and Pascal starts grumbling. He's dropped the little plastic box and is feeling around on the floor for the earplugs he can't do without. After a few minutes, he finds two, a pink one and a yellow one, and stands up triumphantly. Thank goodness. I give him the thumbs-up to show that I'm happy for him. I don't want things to get out of hand—the whole point of the evening is for him to have a good time. He needs to keep his spirits up. And nothing keeps spirits up like a good concert.

When the band comes out on stage, yelling things in English I can't decipher, Pascal shoves the little pieces of polyurethane mousse so far into his ears that I wonder if he can even hear the music. But since he's bobbing his head in rhythm, I figure at least the bassline must make it past the neon filters to his brain.

After forty-five nearly solid minutes of rock and roll, I hear a speaker bust and think the guy is playing way too loud. Even the guitarist is looking around, trying to find the broken amp. But the popping sound keeps coming, and I think it's strange that several speakers have all given up the ghost at once. Pascal hasn't noticed anything—those earplugs must do a damn good job.

And then it's like a chain reaction, almost in slow motion. When the musicians scurry off like rabbits, I realize something's gone wrong. Seriously fucking wrong.

Suddenly, there's a stampede. My mind flashes to a surreal comparison with the scene in *The Lion King* where the animals all flee the valley as fast as they can to save their hides. I can't even count the number of times I watched that movie with my daughter when she was little . . . So many times she actually managed to wear out the tape.

The crowd's movements are totally disorganized, and we're pushed forward toward the stage without understanding what's going on. Some people are lying on top of each other, others trip as they try to make their way through the mass, and still others collapse onto the floor with a thud like rag dolls.

I push Pascal, who's staring at me expectantly, as if he thinks I somehow have all the answers. I shove him forcefully to the ground and throw myself over him, my hands around my head, as if that could protect me from anything. My head is resting on Pascal's. Neither of us says a single word. He's hiding his face in the crook of his arm to keep from seeing people drop to the floor one by one, to keep from seeing the blood, which is all too visible now that the lights are back on.

I've finally figured out that these sickos are hunting us, that they're taking us down like game. But I have no idea why. My mind keeps churning, trying to answer why, but I keep coming up empty. There must be some mistake. A prank? A game of some sort? What the hell is going on? It's been going on too long to be a targeted vendetta . . .

The shots become less frequent. From the corner of my eye, I see shadows stand up and then fall right back down. Pascal and I don't move a muscle. We play dead.

And we wait. A long time.

I close my eyes, concentrating on the shots, trying to figure out how far they are from us. The sharp scent of gunpowder fills the room, and I think it's strange that I know exactly what it is even though I've never smelled it before.

The shooters—there must be several of them since the firing is all around us—are no longer showering the crowd with bullets. They're finishing people off one by one at point-blank range. When it sounds like footsteps are getting nearer, inside I'm screaming, *Not me! Oh Jesus, please not me!* And when they move away, I can't help but feel relieved. Every time a gun is fired, I take a deep breath, realizing we're not hit. I know that means someone else was, but I don't give a shit. I just want to save myself and Pascal. He is going to hate me for bringing him here tonight. Some distraction!

I inconspicuously pull the neon-yellow earplug out of his ear and whisper, "Better than the trucks, huh?" I can tell he's smiling.

I have to protect him, whatever it takes. I'm the one who brought him here, and I'm the one who's going to get him out. Period. The shots get closer and I tense up, like a statue. I hold my breath and adopt a vacant look. Someone kicks my calf, hard, then my thigh, and finally my hip. I clench my jaw and contract all my muscles. I don't make a single sound. I don't even exhale.

Unexpectedly, as shots continue to fire, I start to get angry, despite my fear of dying here like a dog. I want to jump up and use the element of surprise to rip the Kalashnikov from the guy's hands, then punch him in the gut and bash his head in with the stock. I want to be a hero; I want that with all my heart, but instead I'm just some loser lying on the floor hoping that playing dead will keep him alive, praying to make it out of here, to win this gruesome game of hide-and-seek. I think of those men in the Thalys train from Amsterdam to Paris who tackled their assailant and disarmed him a few months ago. I wonder what would have happened if they hadn't taken that risk, if they'd hesitated, and I'm ashamed not to be more like them. I'm ashamed to be a coward, ashamed of staying down when these sick bastards are shooting like this is some damn video game. I'm ashamed not to have the guts to get up and fight when I know that in this crowd, we're the older and wiser ones. That was clear when we walked in: this place is full of kids. They should be able to count on me. I'm ashamed and scared. I don't have the balls to take the risk, much less to sacrifice myself. In some ways, it's reassuring to know that nobody is brave enough to do it, that we're all cowering like rats, waiting to be shot, praying to be saved.

The footsteps move away again, and I ask Pascal if he's doing all right.

"Just great, man . . . ," he whispers.

I'm relieved to know he's still alive. I hear someone far away from us, a young woman, I think, start crying softly. A wail of anguish or pain, it's hard to tell. Annoyed, everyone shushes her in unison, as if they were at the movies and some overly talkative broad was keeping them from enjoying the show. As if they were hushing a noisy brat in a classroom. The girl's sobbing now, almost silently. Then there's a barrage of bullets, and she stops. Is she holding back from fear of getting shot? Have they finished her off? I have no idea, but she's quiet now.

Suddenly, at the other end of the room, a voice shouts, "They're going upstairs!" A group of people next to us stand up and start running, stepping over unmoving bodies, dead or alive. I decide it's time to get the hell out of here, that soon we'll be in a café drinking beer, talking about the hell of a night we've had. We'll slap ourselves on the back, laugh a bit too loud to ease our nerves, and wonder if maybe it's all too absurd to have been anything other than a bad dream.

I squeeze Pascal's shoulder, to let him know as discreetly as possible that it's time to move. Only a yard from where we're standing, a couple struggles to their feet. The man is holding the woman by her waist as she limps, looking like a marionette he's pulling awkwardly along behind him by the strings.

The hail of gunfire starts up again. I don't know where it's coming from. The couple slumps to the floor before my eyes, mowed down like bowling pins. Pascal and I hit the deck immediately. All of a sudden, I don't feel like laughing anymore—I never really felt like it, actually, it's just a stupid expression. I'm starting to think we're not going to make it out of here, that they're going to take us all out one by one until the floor is covered in dead bodies. Bang, bang, bang, like a goddamn game of whack-a-mole.

We'd better keep our heads down.

"Hold on, Pascal. We'll make it out of here, don't worry." I feel his head nod under mine, and I continue, "I'm sure the cops are about to bust in here and get the bastards. It's gonna be okay. They'll take them down real quick, you'll see."

He doesn't say anything, but he's shaking. His body is trembling so violently, it's almost like a vibrating cell phone.

"Shh, hang on, okay? Hang on, I'm here. I'm right here . . ."

I keep whispering without stopping, the same thing over and over, to reassure him, to reassure myself. I can feel him calming down, his muscles slowly relaxing.

"It'll be over soon, shh . . ."

3

SOFIANE

Of course, by the time I get there, the place is already full of people jammed in tight. Given the dense crowd, I know instantly there's no way I'll ever make it down to the stage.

I order a Coke at the bar and stand there a few minutes, trying to determine the most strategic spot. I quickly decide the balcony is my best shot; I won't be in the heart of the action, but at least I'll have a good view. And from there, I'll probably be able to film a few songs with my phone.

When I get upstairs, I head toward the front to look out over the fans below: a preteen boy carrying his girlfriend on his shoulders, even though there's nothing to see on stage yet; a redheaded woman waving her hand wildly in the air, probably trying to find someone in the crowd; two older men who've managed to make their way toward the front. One of them is wearing a wide-brimmed cowboy hat—the people behind him must be thrilled.

I send Héloïse a text: I miss you! It's really too bad we don't have the same taste in music. I've always thought it would be fun to go to more concerts together. I barely have the time to stuff my phone back into my jeans pocket before it beeps with an incoming message. I miss you too. Can't wait until you get home to help finish the favors! Very funny. The lights dim, and I put my cell on vibrate.

Seven songs I know by heart, then chaos.

The pit starts writhing frantically, like weeping willows in a storm. Explosions, the smell of gunpowder wafting up to our nostrils in the balcony, the suddenly deserted stage, blinding flashes in the dark.

And the screaming.

I instinctively dive behind a row of red velvet seats, like dozens of other people around me. I wait for the shooting to stop, but the barrage only pauses for a few seconds, then gets going again, even louder. A little voice in my head whispers that I really should have stayed home and done origami with Héloïse.

Below, the gunfire continues relentlessly. The screams echoing through the air become increasingly rare. People keep quiet, or can no longer speak. A terrifying silence envelops the building, as if time has stopped.

On the floor in front of me, bodies start crawling, and I realize I can't stay here. They—not that I know who "they" are—will come upstairs eventually. They'll climb the steps and take us out one by one. It's raining bullets on the ground floor, and I know they'll come for us too. So I follow the others through the rows of padded seats, making as little noise as possible.

When I've crawled a few yards, I see a door. I crouch and run doubled over, protecting my head with my hands, toward the exit. People push and shove, fighting to survive, like stampeding wild animals. When I finally make it past the door, I realize that it's just a tiny little room, barely a dozen square feet. No emergency exit, no stairs down to the ground floor. We're trapped. All the gunmen have to do is come up the stairs and open the door to finish us off. How many machine gun bursts does it take to wipe out forty people? Two? One, if the shooter aims well?

I watch, unmoving, as two men try to barricade the door with an old couch. Their efforts seem so futile, ridiculous even. A sofa as our last line of defense against assault rifles.

There is a door at the far end of the little room, but the glimmer of hope is quickly stamped out. Restrooms. Fucking restrooms that lead nowhere. Somebody is desperately trying to break through the drop-ceiling tiles. I watch as the white material crumbles. I feel like it's making a hell of a lot of noise, like we're going to attract the shooters' attention. One by one, we climb up into the black hole that leads who knows where, probably nowhere. I bump into metal beams and choke back groans of pain. There are piles of dust everywhere, and I fight to keep from coughing, or at least keep my mouth shut when I do.

Everyone freezes and we stay hidden there in the dark, on the lookout. There are about ten of us up here in this makeshift attic, listening as the shooters make their way to the balcony, hearing their footsteps on the stairs. Apparently the soundproofing in the building isn't so great. Nobody moves.

They'll open the door, push the couch out of the way, make their way to the bathroom, and see the hole in the ceiling. It'll take them only a few seconds to figure out we're hiding up here. They'll riddle us with bullets, shoot blindly through the ceiling, and we'll be blown to bits, like clay pigeons at a skeet competition.

I close my eyes and focus on the sounds around me. Footsteps, screams, explosions, groans, blows, begging. All my senses are wired, on high alert.

The minutes tick by sluggishly. My lungs are on fire and I pray silently, to whoever might be listening, not to have an asthma attack. I'm scared shitless and, more than anything else, I feel so, so alone. So trapped. I want to grab hold of someone, anyone, but I repress the urge. I try to meet someone's gaze. In vain.

I think of Héloïse, who must be busy meticulously counting her white and silver candies. With one hand, I pull my phone out of my pocket and quickly type out a message. I'm sorry I haven't helped you more with the wedding. I love you, you know. I see others doing the same, the darkness dotted with an artificial glow, faces momentarily lit up. A minute later, she answers, Being sorry doesn't cut it. You're going to have to make up for it over the next three months!

Apparently Héloïse has no idea what's going on. Suddenly I wonder if anyone outside knows what's happening here. If the rest of the world knows. Or if we're all alone, left to our own devices.

I decide not to worry her. What good would it do? I want to write something poetic and romantic that she'll remember in case . . . in case she never sees me again. But I can't think of anything. I've never been good with words, and my current situation isn't helping me channel my inner Shakespeare. You've got all my evenings from now until February to work on anything you like. Not exactly inspired, but I don't want to write anything too flowery either, because it would cue her in to the fact that I'm in danger. Her reply is almost instantaneous: Stop or I'll swoon! I smile, and she sends another message: Hasn't your concert started yet? My fingers fly over the screen. Yeah, but it's far from the best I've seen. I cling to my sense of humor, even though I don't feel like laughing at all. If I could, I'd call my parents, but there's no way I could talk or even whisper on the phone. Too dangerous.

The footsteps seem to be getting closer, and I hear shouting, then people screaming and bullets silencing them. We all turn our phones off at once, as if on cue, and I can feel fear mounting in each of us. My left leg has fallen asleep, but I don't dare change positions.

I wait, my senses straining.

I stifle the urge to check the time on my phone. I feel like the minutes are dragging on, like we're in an alternate dimension. Is it still Friday, will the sun rise soon, how long have we been here, waiting, watching, biting our nails, saying our good-byes in our heads while praying to be saved?

Outside, sirens are blaring. Ambulances and police, I hope. Hurry up. I'm afraid the ceiling is going to collapse and that we'll fall onto the gunmen, afraid that someone might sneeze and get us caught. I feel like an animal backed into a corner. A mouse hoping that the cats will soon tire of their game.

For a fraction of a second, I go deaf. There's been an explosion, and I'm sure the whole building's going to collapse, that we're going to be blown to dust, without even trying to escape. Then, a second explosion. I grab hold of a small beam, as if it were somehow sturdier than the walls or floor. Then yet another boom—I feel it throughout my body and am left shaking, unable to move.

Below, a chorus of voices, a parade of footsteps.

I close my eyes again and focus on the sounds. Waiting for something to happen.

We're saved. At last.

When I climb down, I lift my hands up high in the air so they won't think I'm a terrorist and shoot me by mistake. The cops—all dressed like Robocop—must be pretty tense, so I want it to be very clear I'm not a criminal. I walk slowly, no sudden movements. I'm so afraid of catching a bullet now, just as this nightmare is so close to over. I walk back through the room we barricaded ourselves in, the balcony, the stairs down to the ground floor. I concentrate on the tips of my sneakers, the sound of my own footsteps. I try not to see, not to look around. I walk through blood, through shapeless pieces of flesh, but my eyes stay focused on my feet moving forward, in step with the police officer who's escorting us.

As I walk through the glass door, which isn't really a door anymore, my phone vibrates in my pocket, making me jump. A text from Héloïse.

Damn it, Sofiane, you said you'd be home by midnight.

4

Bastien

In the end, I invite Leïla to come with me to the concert, and she accepts without a second thought, thrilled to have the chance to see the concert for free.

In the quickly growing line in front of the Bataclan, all the guys turn around to check out her amazing figure. We've known each other since high school, so I've gotten used to the effect she has on men, even if I can't help but wish some of those looks were for me. There's something magnetic about Leïla, though she never seems to notice. I know I'm being sized up, evaluated by the other guys who are wondering if we're a couple or if they might have a shot tonight.

Once we get inside, we hurry toward the stage. The Bataclan isn't very big, so if we want to get a good spot, we can't dawdle at the coat check. After thirty minutes of chatting as we wait, Leïla wrinkles her nose like a little girl caught red-handed.

"Don't tell me you have to pee!"

"No, it's not that . . . It's just so hot in here, I need something to drink. We're crammed in so tight, it's suffocating!"

"But we'll never make it back to the front row if we leave now!"

"I can go to the bar by myself if you want to stay. I'll try to make it back . . . ," she says with a cajoling smile. As usual, she wins me over.

"No, let's go. I'll come too. I don't want you to die of thirst."

We slowly elbow our way through the crowd to the bar, assailed by groaning from malcontents who somehow expect to make it through a concert without anyone brushing up against them.

"What do you want?" Leïla asks me.

"Nothing, thanks. I'm not thirsty."

While she's ordering a beer from the bartender, I notice a thirty-something guy waiting to pay for his plastic cup of Coke. He has a short brown beard, a thin nose, and dark eyes that make me want to say something smart to break the ice. It only takes me a few seconds to realize he must be a serious fan of the band: he's wearing a black Eagles of Death Metal T-shirt with a huge green skull sporting a mustache and sunglasses—a design I didn't see at the stand near the entrance.

As I'm trying to muster the courage to casually talk to him, the bartender hands him his change, and his long legs take him quickly up the stairs to the balcony. My prey has escaped before I could even open my mouth.

"Are we staying here?" Leïla asks teasingly. She must have enjoyed watching my internal turmoil.

We take a few steps away from the bar to get a good view of the whole stage. The lights finally dim and the music really gets going.

We're among the first to realize that the cracks and pops we keep hearing aren't part of the show, and that they're not coming from firecrackers or a fight. Because we're at the very back of the venue, when we turn around at the first shot, we see what's going on right behind us.

A few yards from me, I see a guy around my age, not more than twenty. Dark skin, black hair, sharp eyes. He's waving his AK-47 around in circles, shooting down into the pit. The movement is methodical, calm, as persistent as a sprinkler watering grass. A bit farther from us, I can see other shadows doing the same thing. I think to myself that they seem to be incredibly well prepared. They're not rushed at all—on the contrary. It's like they know that, at this exact moment, they're all-powerful. That nothing and no one can stop them or resist. Their composure is astounding, because it makes it seem like what's happening is normal—minus the screaming and the sound of running feet—instead of completely surreal.

The crowd is disorganized, chaotic, hysterical.

My legs are paralyzed. I can't act. I feel like I'm watching the scene from above. My brain feels dead, and it's only when I meet the determined gaze of the guy holding the assault rifle that I snap back to reality. With what looks like a smile on his face, he coolly trains his gun on me.

Then, at last, I turn and run. I see Leïla ahead of me, sprinting. I dive onto a pile of people lying on the floor and crawl over their bodies despite the groans and wailing that grow louder. I keep climbing, without a destination. I hear bullets whistle past, all around me, I feel something, or rather someone, fall hard onto my legs. I try to pull myself out using my arms, but the weight on my thighs and calves is too heavy.

I realize the gunfire is getting closer and immediately stop moving.

Thoughts are flying through my head, no longer under my control, like they're talking among themselves, independent of my wishes: *Not now, not like this!* and then a conflicted feeling of almost serene acceptance—*I'm going to die. This is the end*—a strange impression of resigned well-being that disappears as quickly as it comes. *There's no way I'm going to die here, for no reason at all!* Defiance overwhelms me and a primal anger takes over. If I'm going to die, I'd rather it be as I try to escape than as I cower here in a pile of dead bodies still warm from the life seeping out of them. I move my legs around a bit, discreetly, to keep them from going numb. I close my eyes and fight the disagreeable tingling that warns me they're falling asleep. Inch by inch, I manage to pull myself out from under the body slumped over me.

When the shots move away, toward the other side of the pit, I take advantage of the distance to get up and run, stepping over or trampling other people. Despite my best efforts, I trip on an obstacle—an arm, a leg?—and fall flat on my stomach in a dark, lukewarm puddle on the floor. The hail of bullets moves back toward me and I freeze, feeling the blood of less fortunate people soak into my clothes. Because I've been lucky so far—obviously, since I'm still alive, and no bullet has pierced my skin.

I stay alert, vigilant, and the next time things go quiet, I'm already in the starting blocks. I run—no, I fly for my life. I look in vain for the exit. I'm like hunted prey, like a wasp trying to find an open window or a sparrow banging into walls hoping to miraculously escape. With everyone pushing and shoving, the halls are like a labyrinth. I used to have a recurring nightmare about a house with burgundy-red walls, where I ran and ran without ever finding a door. I would try to escape, but always, I inevitably ended up back where I'd started. Then I would wake up and fight my hardest not to fall back to sleep too quickly. I'd like to tell myself that I'm going to wake up, and that when I do I'll grope around to turn on my bedside lamp, and the fear will evaporate as quickly as it built up. In the meantime, I keep pushing through other people, hurrying toward any possible exit.

I finally stumble upon an open door and take refuge inside what looks to be a dressing room. There's no way outside, and the shots continue to echo beyond the door. I hesitate. Should I hide or go back out in hopes I'll finally find the emergency exit? Other people come in behind me and close the door. We all glance at one another, terrified. I huddle in a corner of the room, as far from the door as possible. There's nothing to block the door with. A girl with a long neck turns out the lights, and we find ourselves sitting in the dark, listening to the muffled sound of gunfire through the walls.

And now the waiting begins. Leïla isn't here, and as I finally manage to catch my breath, terrifying images ruthlessly assail my consciousness. Please tell me she made it out, that she's still alive . . .

The few other people in the room with me immediately pull out their phones, and I hear their fingers dashing across the screens, their hushed voices on the verge of tears.

I grab my phone from the pocket of my too-tight pants and dial my mother. One ring, two, three, four . . . *Come on, Mom, pick up . . .* Her voicemail answers, but doesn't even provide the reassurance of her voice. A metallic recording chimes, "The person you're trying to reach is currently unavailable," and I hang up. The screen of my HTC tells me it's 10:11 p.m., and I realize that my mother is probably lying comfortably in her bed, while her phone has most certainly been left behind, forgotten somewhere downstairs. I try the landline, even though I hate to wake her up with a start and scare her—no one ever calls our house after eight o'clock.

After three endless rings, someone finally picks up. I hear my father's gruff voice, ready to bark at the idiot who has dared bother him so late at night. Just as I'm about to speak, I hear footsteps approaching, then they stop right in front of the door. There's a motionless shadow in the sliver of light coming through the crack at the bottom. The shooting continues amid the deathly silence. Outside, a breathless voice screams, "Please, I beg you . . . ," and a volley silences it without further ado.

I hear my father proffering increasingly annoyed hellos in my ear. I can't answer him, not with a gunman on the hunt just a few steps away. "You think you're real funny, huh?" I focus on his distant voice and choke back my hiccups of terror. "Most people are sleeping at this time of night, you know!" I duck my head to my knees, make myself as small and compact as possible, wishing I had a shell to protect me, like a turtle. "Hello? Hello? Can you hear me?"

I hear you, Dad. I hear you, even though I can't answer. Don't hang up, please, please don't. Talk to me, talk about whatever you want, but keep talking.

There's a deafening crash as the door bursts open and light suddenly fills the dressing room. On the other end of the line, I hear my father letting rip with "Are you gonna keep this up long, this silent game?"

5

Léopold

The Bataclan is small, almost cozy, but as a result, it's already sweltering inside. I quickly tie my sweatshirt around my waist while doing my best to follow Alex, Tiago, and Sylvain in a single-file line toward the stage.

"Wouldn't it be awesome to play here, guys?"

My three friends nod vigorously in agreement. I take out my phone to snap a picture of the four of us with the stage and its collection of different-sized amps in the background.

"Maybe one day we'll be the ones everyone comes to see!"

I wave my arm around in enthusiastic emphasis and accidentally hit the face of a young guy trying to edge his way forward. He rubs his silver-hoop-clad ear, grimacing in pain. I offer a lame apology, and he smiles—clearly not one to hold a grudge. He glances at my arm and shouts, "Nice tattoo!" as he studies the octopus poking happily out from under my T-shirt. His girlfriend, a voluptuous brunette, is waiting for him a few steps ahead, and he hurries to catch up with her.

I take advantage of the fact that the lights are still on to post the photo I've just taken to our band's Facebook page, with the caption, "Tonight we're in the audience!" The huge guy next to me is watching, clearly curious. He's so tall and massive that he reminds me of the hero from *The Green Mile*. I'm sure he could crush my phone to pieces in the palm of his hand without breaking a sweat, without even feeling a thing. I make a mental note not to mosh with him. Too dangerous.

When Jesse Hughes sings the first words of "Save a Prayer," one of my favorites from the latest album, I take out my cell and dial my best friend, Stan, who lives near Bordeaux and couldn't make it tonight. I can't hear it ringing, but I can see on the screen that he's picked up. I scream, "This is for you, dude!" into my iPhone, then hold it up above my head so he can hear what he's missing. I'm sure he's put his phone on speaker and is swaying alone in his living room, wishing he were here with us.

Sylvain is having fun playing the solos on air guitar, and Alex is crowd surfing a few rows in front of us, carried by the outstretched arms of the ecstatic audience. Tiago is giving his all in a particularly energetic moshing style—not everyone's piece of cake. I do my best to anchor my feet to the ground and avoid being carried away by the undulating crowd.

Less than fifteen minutes later, the crowd stops swaying and lurches, seized by a wave of panic that's spreading at lightning speed.

Threatening silhouettes bark, "Allahu Akbar," and in the split second it takes me to turn around, the massive John Coffey doppelganger topples down onto me, throwing me to the floor.

I wish I'd thought fast enough to bolt. I feel people climbing and crawling over me, then everything slows in an eerie silence. It's like I'm underwater—everything takes longer, seems heavier.

Bullets are flying and, given the number of bodies falling to the ground, they're hitting their targets. I want to get out of here, but moving—even the slightest twitch—is clearly out of the question.

With each volley of gunfire, I feel the ground vibrate under my cheek, stomach, and palms, all pressed to the floor. I'm like a tracker in a Western, ear to the tracks listening for a coming train. But the train's already here, and I can't tell if my body is trembling with fear or if it's shaking in wake of the blasts. It takes all my strength, but I slowly free my legs from beneath the unmoving body that's cutting off my circulation. Gently, inch by inch. Avoid drawing attention. I have to get out before my legs go numb.

I lock eyes with a woman only a yard from me. I've never seen so much helplessness, fear, and silent pleading in a single expression. I stare back at her and try to telepathically communicate that it'll all be okay, that she'll make it out of here, that this has to stop soon. That the cops are going to burst in and shut these guys down within minutes—they have to. This is definitely the first time I've ever really hoped the police would show up somewhere.

I stay like that for an eternity, losing all sense of time. I let myself drown in her eyes, focus on them like a lighthouse in the night. For now, we're alive.

Even amid the chaos, it occurs to me that, under better circumstances, this girl could be just my type, with her big, wide eyes, and ebony hair fanned out on the floor around her. Under better circumstances, I probably would have struck up an awkward conversation by asking her where to find the restroom while my friends mocked me loudly. I could have asked her to have a drink with me, all the while afraid she'd turn me down disdainfully. I might have run my fingers through my hair—always tastefully disheveled—to boost my confidence. I could have told her I'm a drummer in an awesome rock band, counting on the fact that musicians always get the girl. She would have smiled shyly instead of staring at me, imploring me to save her. She would have laughed at the jokes I attempted to make, blushed when I complimented her, when I told her just how pretty and attractive I found her. Who knows, maybe after the concert she would have given me her phone number, scrawling it on my palm with an old Bic pen she'd unearth from the bottom of her overflowing purse. I'd tell myself she must have given me a fake number, that when I'd call the next day, I'd realize that it wasn't hers at all, that I was on the phone with some gruff guy with such a deep voice there was no room for doubt. But I would have been wrong, and when she'd pick up the phone, I would have heard the impatience in her voice, which she would have tried to disguise with feigned indifference, and I would have casually asked her to dinner sometime. I wouldn't have said *tonight*, to avoid seeming over-eager, and she would have told me that she had a free evening the following week, so as not to seem desperate. We would have seen each other again, both of us a bit clumsy and tense, afraid to disappoint or seem unlikable, afraid of not being as attractive as in the dim lights of the Bataclan. It could have been the beginning of something.

I've already come up with a whole story with this girl, and I don't even know her name. I keep my eyes on her and feel like I could almost forget what's going on around us. Suddenly Tiago shakes my arm and whispers that it's now or never—they're reloading and we have to go, quick. I stand halfway up and see the shooter rifling through his backpack, probably looking for more ammunition. He's got his Kalashnikov under his arm, and I notice it's held together with duct tape. I can't help but think sarcastically that their budget must have been too tight for new guns. Several groups of people start moving, half-running, half-crawling in a haphazard choreography. I'm about to go too when I look back. The black-haired girl is still lying on the floor, watching me wordlessly, even more terrified than before. I whisper at her to get up and come with me, but she very gently shakes her head against the floor, without moving any other part of her body.

I hear a loud click and realize the hail of gunfire is about to start up again. I've missed my chance.

I lie back down, without taking my eyes off my silent confidante. After all we've been through, after the whole story I've invented for us, I couldn't have left her behind anyway.

I smile sadly at her, and we wait.

For now, we're alive.

6

MARGOT

The lights are already out and the music blaring when we finally make it inside, sweating from the run from the République Metro stop. After we quickly check our coats, William suggests we stay near the bar, behind the roiling pit, but I insist we go up to the balcony, and he gives in to make me happy.

The seats upstairs are all taken, so William heads to the banister to watch the band from above. The crowd is amped up and I'm glad we're not down in the pit, getting bumped and jostled from all sides. At the end of the song, the guitarist throws something to the audience—probably a guitar pick—and I see a tattooed arm reach out to catch the precious object. From back here, it looks like the guy has an octopus covering his entire arm, and I wonder how someone gets the crazy idea to permanently mark their body with that. Do octopuses symbolize something?

I miraculously manage to find an empty seat in the front row and drag William along with me. The people behind us grumble, and I try to make myself as small as possible, half-sitting on my husband's lap. If the babysitter hadn't canceled at the last minute, we'd have been on time and would have had no problem getting two seats . . .

Suddenly William jumps up and leans over the banister. I don't even have time to realize anything out of the ordinary is happening, until I see him slump and fall over the side. I stand up, screaming, and see the crowd below swaying bizarrely. Dozens of people drop like dominoes. My terrified cry stops short in my throat when I finally realize that there are madmen downstairs shooting into the crowd of cowering bodies.

Someone pulls me backward, hard, and pushes me into a seated position behind the red seats. Everything is muffled, the sound of my heartbeat echoing in my temples nearly drowning out the screams and the shots. I stay put, shaken to the core, unable to find any words for what I've just seen, for what's happened and is still happening. I know William isn't next to me anymore, but I don't understand how he could have disappeared so suddenly, without a scream or a sound.

All around me I feel people crawling, almost submissively, politely, but I'm fixed to the spot—it's all become too absurd, too unreal for me to act.

Once again, someone—the same person or someone else?—takes hold of my shoulders and makes me get onto my hands and knees. I hear whispering, but can't make out the meaning: "We have to go," "We can't stay here." I have only one thing in my mind: *Where is William?* Is it possible this whole thing is just some twisted practical joke, worthy of *The Game*? If I stood up right now, would he be standing over there, motioning at me to join him? Could this all simply be a hallucination, a terrible nightmare?

A shadowy figure shakes me, again and again, like some limp rag doll, then slaps me, harder and harder, until my eyes finally connect with the ones across from me. A man in glasses is staring at me. He holds my face tight between the palms of his hands.

"You can't stay here, understand?" he urges.

I don't answer. My lips seem to be sealed, sewn together.

"Do you have children?" he asks.

Do you have children? The short sentence ricochets around the inside of my skull like a pool ball until it finally makes sense.

It brings me back to the surface. I open my mouth, in need of oxygen, and grab hold of the stranger's wrists.

Sacha.

I finally manage to get to my knees and start moving, trying to escape. Then, without knowing why, I collapse onto the floor, unable to move. A dull pain is radiating from my lower abdomen, and when I instinctively run my hand over it, I feel that my dress is soaked. Panic rushes through my veins, like an electrical shock.

"You can make it, I won't leave you!"

I keep going, half-crawling, half-carried by this man I've never seen before, who seems determined to do whatever it takes to save me.

Sacha.

I can picture his cheerful face, his long eyelashes that will make all the girls fall for him in a dozen or so years, his little arms that reach out for me as soon as I come into his line of sight.

When I pause to catch my breath and look around, I see dozens of people huddled together, eyes to the ceiling as if they're expecting a helicopter to drop a rope down to save them. I glance up to see what's attracted their attention. A skylight and a glimpse of dark sky. That's our beacon of hope? People are giving each other boosts, but I stay seated, doing nothing. The bespectacled stranger won't give up on me, and ties his heather-gray scarf around my stomach, so tight it feels like he's a saleswoman trying to convince me that, yes, I *can* fit into a size 4.

"Women and children first," says a voice, and I suddenly want to laugh—it's all so grotesque. We're on the *Titanic*, we've hit an iceberg, and our lifeboat is this skylight. So far away and so high up that there's no way I'm getting through it. None. My legs have fallen asleep and I feel light-headed. One by one, they help each other up, arms outstretched so that strangers can pull them into the Parisian sky from above.

"You have to stand up. I know it's hard, but you can do it."

I want to tell him to let it go, that there's no point. But then I hear Sacha's distant voice from his crib, static on the baby monitor, then *Ma-ma-ma*, which I like to interpret as *Mama*. I have to go to him before he starts crying, before he starts to think we've abandoned him. The longer he waits, the harder it is to calm him down, to reassure him. *I'm coming, sweetie, Mommy's coming, shh . . .*

I'm shaky, but the man helps me up. I'd like to tell him how sorry I am to have ruined his scarf—I'm sure it's cashmere—and that I'll buy him a new one. I know this little store in the Marais that has lovely things. I feel like I'm floating, like nothing matters anymore, and I let myself be led along as if I were drunk.

Several people work together to lift me up. Everyone's fussing over me; I almost feel like the Queen of Sheba on her throne. Then more arms grab me, pull me up, and I forget where I am, tossed about, unable to do anything for myself. The pain in my stomach is spreading, dull and throbbing. It's so bad I can't feel it anymore. It's a strange, inexplicable feeling: hurting so much I don't hurt anymore. It's like the pain is taking over, my body disappearing, fading into it.

The skylight leads to the roof, where I can make out several figures in the dark. Someone lays me down.

"Stay here, I'll be back," they say. I smile—as if there were any risk I'd disappear into the night. "Whatever you do, don't fall asleep. Hold on."

I suddenly realize Sacha's not crying anymore. Maybe he fell asleep? He must have found his thumb and sucked it to soothe himself. I better get to bed soon too, since Sacha always gets up at six and I don't even know what *sleep in* means anymore. Yeah, if I want to be well rested, I have to get to sleep too. Tomorrow will be another long day. I feel so tired all of a sudden.

Somebody's pushing on my stomach, but I don't know why. People are gathering around me, but nothing makes sense. It reminds me of my labor with Sacha: the epidural was too strong, everything hazy. These people are all slurring their words, and now they're fuzzy, so fuzzy. Their voices are like echoes in the mountains, their syllables bouncing around, lengthening with every word. I listen to the multicolored sounds as they spring forth, grow louder, then slowly fade away.

Now, Sacha is right next to me. His baby smell—a cloying blend of shampoo and spit-up—fills my nostrils, and I suddenly feel light.

It's cold and the hairs on my arms stand on end. But there's no wind, not even the slightest breeze, just shadows dancing above me, singing a strange, discordant melody, keeping me from drifting off peacefully. Could I have forgotten to do something before going to bed? I've got that annoying feeling that I've missed something. But just as I almost put my finger on it, it slips away again, leaving my hand pitifully empty.

My eyelids struggle to open a sliver, and I notice the stars in the black sky. It was a really good idea that William had to stick them to the ceiling in Sacha's room. The tiny glowing lights sparkle weakly. The overhead light must have been out for a while now, but time always flies when I camp out next to Sacha's crib to get him to sleep. He's snoring softly next to me, and the sound of his breath lulls me like the sound of waves rushing in and out. I close my eyes and peacefully embrace the moment.

I'm not going to spend the whole night in his room. I'll just stay until his breathing is deep and steady—the moment when I know he won't startle when I get up. A hand strokes my face, sweeping gently over my forehead. Must be William coming to wake me. *You've fallen asleep again, honey!* I hear indistinct whispering and want to place my index finger on my lips to tell him to be quiet—it took so long to get Sacha settled. He takes me in his arms, and I hear my son turn over in the crib, his sleep sack rustling against the fitted sheet. I don't even need to open my eyes to know exactly what position he's in now. On his back, hands level with his head, lips slightly parted. He's finally surrendered, so peaceful.

7

Daphné

I rush up Boulevard Voltaire, almost running, since I'm on the verge of being late—as usual. I barely had time to close my register and whip off my bright-red uniform, which is too tight in the waist, before dashing out the door to my second job. The coat check at the Bataclan is waiting for me, along with a line of concert-goers standing outside the building's outlandish Asian-inspired façade.

Doriane is already there, obviously, and even though she never says anything when I'm late, the simple fact that she's always there first makes me feel guilty. It makes me feel slightly better to remember she's a student, that she doesn't have another job or a child to manage in addition to her own life, but in the end I can't help but envy her carefree punctuality. Being on time is disturbingly easy for her. For most people, even. Sometimes I wonder if I'm the only one always running, always trying to beat the clock.

I nod sheepishly at my coworker—already standing tall, ready to welcome the first people in line to drop off their things—then hurry to the break room to put away my own: a bunched-up trench coat and a tattered leather purse. I race back to the counter and assume the most affable face I can manage.

Audience members file by for the next two hours, leaving their coats, sweaters, purses, or sometimes even shopping bags from a preconcert spree. The regulars recognize me and smile; the others simply slap their things down on the counter. When the line begins to dwindle, Doriane and I can finally talk.

"I didn't think you'd be working tonight."

"Really, why?"

"It's your birthday, isn't it? I would've thought you'd have someone cover for you so you could celebrate with your family!"

"Actually, my husband threw a surprise party for me last night! Planned the whole thing," I explain as I put a worn camouflage jacket on a hanger.

"Wow! No way my boyfriend would ever do anything like that. Sounds like you've found a great guy!"

The concert's been going for a few minutes, so I have to raise my voice for Doriane to hear me. We're interrupted by a young woman asking how much it will cost to leave her purse and coat. Doriane answers, and the blond man who's with the woman clears his throat.

"Are you sure you want to leave your things, Margot? We'll have to wait in line to get them back afterward . . ."

"I know it's not cheap, but I really don't feel like carrying my coat and bag around all night!"

The man sighs, giving in. Once Doriane has put their things away, they walk away holding hands, hurrying to see the band, which has already played a couple of songs.

"Do you know who's playing tonight?"

"Eagles of Death Metal!" answers my coworker enthusiastically.

"Never heard of them . . ."

Going by name alone, I'm pretty sure my eardrums are in for another trying evening.

◆　◆　◆

When the band is already half an hour into the concert, Doriane goes to smoke a cigarette in front of the entrance, and I stay to staff the counter in case an audience member suddenly decides to get his or her things.

When she comes back in, accompanied by a gust of cool outside air, she takes my place, and I head to the restroom. Out of curiosity, I walk through the back of the auditorium and watch the enthusiastic musicians bouncing around the stage. Their music is more rock than metal, it turns out, though it's still plenty loud.

I hurry to the restrooms on the left side of the venue—though we've gotten in the habit of taking turns once the show's started, there are always supposed to be two of us at the coat check, so it's best not to draw attention to myself.

While I'm washing my hands, the strident sound of audio feedback floods my ears and makes me shiver. These guys aren't very good—everyone in the audience must have just plugged their ears and clenched their jaws. As I leave the restroom, my hands still wet, I see a panicked horde rush past me. I'm thrown back against the wall, stunned.

There must be a fire. Something must have caught fire on stage, a short circuit. There must be a fire in the main auditorium and everyone's trying to escape. They're climbing all over each other to get out, like frightened animals.

For a split second, I think about going to get my purse from the break room. Julien gave it to me when Charline was born, and I love it, even though the leather's become worn and damaged over the years. But the crowd is pushing me backward, and I realize there's no point fighting against the current.

Ahead of me, someone finally manages to open an emergency exit, and a flood of people bursts into the silent alley next to the Bataclan. A few people fall down right in front of me and get trampled, suffocated. It's horrible. Behind me I see a hand reaching up from the ground, grabbing at anything at all to escape the mass of bodies crushing down on its owner. Without thinking, I grab it and pull the arm toward me as hard as I can, but then I feel myself getting dragged down in turn. Instead of saving this person, I'm going to get sucked into the pile, into the pit of writhing, living quicksand.

Instinctively, I let go. The hand keeps trying to grab onto me, but I push it away forcefully. The fingers get hold of my necklace; I feel the nylon string come untied and the tiny beads scatter. I imagine the bright-green dots flutter to the floor in a colorful shower. I hear explosions. Have they just started? The fire must be razing everything in its path. I have to get away from this inferno.

When I was about ten, an entire family died in a house fire in our neighborhood. They got stuck upstairs, and I can still remember the giant orange flames licking the outside walls until they were black. I remember my dad outside in the street, in pajamas with his too-short garden hose. And the German shepherd, who managed to get out of the family's house because he must have been sleeping in the garage, was sitting on their front lawn howling for his owners, helpless and inconsolable. The windowless ruins of the place stood there for years to remind us. I've never slept the same since that night.

I ignore the screams and groans and push toward the emergency exit, now just steps away. Once outside in the fresh air, I head left, toward Boulevard Voltaire, but a man in a hoodie pulls me firmly behind him in the other direction. When I try to fight him off, explaining that I need to get on the Metro at Saint-Ambroise, he yells, "Do you want them to shoot you or what?"

In a daze, I follow the stream of concert-goers that continues to pour out the emergency exit door. I head up the dark alley, skirting the walls. Since everyone else is running, I do too, without knowing why. Since the others seem to be avoiding open spaces, I do the same, without asking questions. I mimic the others, maybe out of instinct. The hooded man's words keep echoing through my skull but they don't make sense. What was he talking about?

When we reach Rue Amelot, people disband and I watch them disappear in all directions into the night, without knowing which way to go myself. I finally decide to get on the Metro at the closest station, even if I have to change trains a few times to get home.

At the turnstile, I realize I don't have anything on me: no coat, no purse. For the first time in my life, I awkwardly jump the gate, glancing back over my shoulder to make sure a ticket inspector isn't rushing my way.

When I sit down in the nearly empty car, the few passengers on board glance at me quizzically. I must look crazy, breathing heavily, and with my unseasonably light shirt and messy hair. I want to tell them I've just escaped a terrible fire, but all of a sudden I'm not sure exactly what I've escaped. After all, I didn't see any flames or smell any smoke, or even feel any heat . . . People were fleeing something, but I don't know for sure what it was.

My hands still trembling, I rest my head on the vibrating wall and try to figure out what's just happened. The dark-blue rectangular signs of two Metro stations fly by, and when I catch a glimpse of my disheveled reflection in the window, it seems to be asking me why I ran until my lungs could burst without knowing what I was running from, and without stopping for a second to help someone else. Flashes of scenes run through my mind: the green beads falling away, the hand shooting up like a periscope out of water, and the crazy guy in the hoodie who dragged me along behind him. I feel like they're all pieces of a puzzle, of a riddle I should be able to solve. Something very simple that I just can't manage to grasp.

When I get home, Julien's pacing the living room. He runs over as soon as he sees me and hugs me so hard my ribs cry out in pain. Without any warning, I burst into tears, accompanied by uncontrollable hiccups.

"I broke the necklace Charline gave me yesterday . . ."

He still doesn't relax his embrace. It's like he wants to suffocate me.

Finally, he whispers, "I'm so happy you made it home. I was so scared when I saw what was happening on TV . . ."

My eyes still brimming with tears, I finally manage to step back and ask him hesitantly if the fire's under control. My husband looks at me, confused.

"What fire?"

8

Théo

When my dad lets go of my hand, I tell myself it'll be easy to find him again, but when I raise my head to look for him, I realize he's not next to me anymore and I start to panic.

It didn't scare me when we heard the explosions, and everyone started screaming and running this way and that—it was like the concert hall had suddenly become a giant ant hill. Have you ever noticed how ants walk and walk without really going anywhere, turning in circles instead of heading directly where they are going? Well, it was just like that. Grown-ups were running everywhere, but I didn't feel like any of them knew what they were doing. Not at all.

But I didn't get scared, because I was with my dad. He took my hand and whispered in my ear, "Everything's gonna be okay, Théo. I'll get us out of here!" He cleared a path through the crowd for us, and I focused on his hand because I was too short to see anything else. I got squished, pushed, and crushed, but I held on, following Dad as if I were waterskiing and he were the boat.

And then my fingers are in a free fall, and I realize he's gone. Disappeared. I spin around, protecting my face with my forearms, like a boxer. No sign of him. I yell, "Dad!" but there's so much noise, so many other voices, that I know it's a lost cause. Where could he have gone?

Suddenly someone lifts me off the floor, picking me up under my arms like a sack of potatoes. I can't see his face, but from his shoes I know it's not my father. His shoes are black and shiny, so shiny I can almost see my reflection in them. Nothing like my dad's red-and-white Pumas. The man puts me down in a corner and whispers, "Don't move, buddy!" then stands up again with his back to me. So I don't move, even though I'd rather be looking for my dad. To be honest, I don't really know what I'm supposed to do—should I listen to this stranger or not?

Since no one's there to tell me otherwise, I stay put behind the man. He sits me down along a wall and covers me with his body. I feel like he's going to suffocate me, and he smells like sweat. I can't see anything now, but I hear fewer people running and screaming, only the sound of firecrackers continues. I don't know if they're really firecrackers, but since I have no idea what else they could be, that's what I'm calling them. Their *rat-tat-tat-tat* never stops. It fills my head so full I feel like my brain is going to explode. So I concentrate on the man's scent to block out the rest. I breathe in deeply, and the mix of deodorant and strong sweat strangely reminds me a bit of Dad.

Later I'll have to remind Dad about the promise he made, because I know him and he has a habit of forgetting our conversations a little too quickly. In the train, I asked him if we could get a real Christmas tree for once this year.

"A real tree?" he repeated, as if he didn't understand what I was asking.

"Yeah, a real tree. I mean, not made of plastic," I clarified.

He raised his eyebrows to demonstrate his lack of enthusiasm, but I wasn't giving up that easily.

"There are lots of stores that give you a gift card if you buy a real tree, so it doesn't really cost much in the end . . ."

I knew that money was always important to Dad, so I started with that. He screwed up his face and pursed his lips, weighing the pros and cons. I launched my counterattack without letting him speak.

"And I promise I'll sweep up the needles every time I come over. And I'll help you throw it out in January!"

My father sized me up, trying to decide if I was trustworthy. It was the perfect moment to deal the final blow.

"Mom and Olivier don't want to get a real one"—I made the saddest face possible—"but if you say no too, it's okay, I'll get over it . . ."

Without missing a beat, I turned away to watch the countryside through the window as our train sped past. Everything was going according to plan—I was sure that bringing up my mom and Olivier would do the trick. Dad is always worried that I'll forget about him, or start liking my stepfather more.

"We'll go pick it out together in a couple of weeks if you really want one," he offered nonchalantly.

I was much too big for a hug, so I smiled and raised my hand for a high-five.

The man in front of me gets up all of a sudden, and I forget about Dad and the Christmas tree. Running legs fly by, and he grabs me to follow them. I have a hard time running as fast as him, so he basically ends up lugging me along with him—it's like walking on the moon.

Even after we reach the street outside, we keep running, and it occurs to me that the farther we go, the harder it's going to be to find my dad. We duck into the courtyard of a building where there are already a bunch people waiting for who knows what.

"Are you okay, buddy?"

I nod. The man looks around, maybe searching for his fiancée or a friend. Suddenly he signals to a group of people in a corner of the courtyard and tries to take me with him. My legs don't budge an inch.

"I'm going to stay here."

"I can't leave you here alone," pleads the man.

Now that I have a few minutes to really look at him, I realize that he's not as old as my dad. He looks about the same age as Uncle Marc, my mom's little brother. He doesn't even have a beard or anything, but he does have a pierced eyebrow.

"I'm not alone, there's my dad!" I exclaim excitedly when I see my dad and his red-and-white sneakers enter the courtyard. Without waiting a second longer, I start running toward him, and the young guy with the piercing heads over to his group of friends, relieved to know I'll be okay.

But when I reach my father, I realize I've made a mistake. The man is wearing the same exact shoes, but it's not my dad. I stop short, and he doesn't even realize I was running toward him. The two-tone Pumas walk past me without pausing, and the stranger reunites with a woman who jumps into his arms and bursts into tears.

Nobody pays any attention to me. Everyone's busy with their own stuff, some talking to each other, others frantically tapping at their phones. I'm invisible.

All of a sudden, I'm cold. I hadn't noticed it until now, but I'm freezing from standing around doing nothing. I wonder where my coat is, then remember the woman with the ponytail who took it to hang it with Dad's. *Is this your first concert? You're a lucky kid! You'll see, the view from the balcony is amazing!* Dad told her there was no point watching a concert sitting in a seat in the balcony, and that we were headed to the pit. The woman seemed surprised. *The crowd can get pretty rowdy down there, you know . . .* But my father brushed her warning aside with a sweep of his hand, like he used to do with Mom. *I'll be right there to protect him. There's nothing to worry about!* I remember that the woman was wearing a different color nail polish on each nail, like a rainbow. Yellow, orange, red, purple, and blue. It was too bad she didn't have room for green—she would have needed six fingers to do it right.

I rub my forearms to warm myself up a bit, but it doesn't work very well. At least I'm wearing two T-shirts, one over the other. Dad bought me one at the stand earlier, before the concert started. I picked out a black one with a yellow hand, the pinky and pointer fingers sticking up. He said it was the rock-and-roll symbol and showed me how to proudly wave my fist in the air with two fingers up. The people waiting in line with us laughed.

All around me, men and women are walking around wrapped in gold aluminum foil, like chocolate Easter bunnies. I figure my father won't be much longer now, so I sit with my back to the frozen wall, pull my knees to my chest, and wait. To pass the time, I count the shoes that come into the cobblestone courtyard, watching out for even the tiniest glimpse of red in my line of sight.

9

LUCAS

The line of people waiting to get in is already long when Anouk and I arrive at the Bataclan. Thanks to Djibril and Jessica, who got here earlier, we cut in a few yards from the end. I pointedly ignore the people who get huffy about our shameless disregard for the line. I mean, we're all going to get in anyway, right?

Anouk pulls out her cell and takes a picture of the two of us in front of the vintage light panel with "Eagles of Death Metal" printed in big black letters. It's very Broadway. She eagerly gets to work posting it on her Facebook page, so the entire world will know where we are tonight.

Once we get inside, Djibril and I grab a few beers at the bar, because a rock concert without beer isn't really a rock concert at all. Anouk rather conspicuously points to a ten-year-old kid trying on a T-shirt three times his size at the merchandise stand.

"Do you want anything?" she asks.

"Nah, the line's way too long. We can go afterward, it'll be easier then."

We laugh as we watch the kid's father teach him to make the sign of the horns.

"When we have one of our own, we'll bring him or her with us to concerts too, okay?" I whisper in Anouk's ear, and she blushes slightly. I know she'd be on board for a baby, even though neither of us is even twenty-five, and she hasn't finished her midwife training yet. As for me, I'm in no hurry, but this girl could be the one—I've known it since the first day we met at the Créteil train station. Her gently mocking smile, the way her tomboy exterior hides her inner sensitivity, her unpretentious ways. A whole host of little things that clicked with me right away. So, yeah, I absolutely want to have a kid with her someday.

"Where do you want to watch from?" Jessica asks Anouk, since she also knows that my girlfriend is hardly at ease in tight spaces.

"Let's get close to the stage! Don't worry about me!"

I share a discreet, knowing glance with Anouk's best friend, but Jessica simply shrugs, seeming to say, *If she's game, then let's not try to figure out why!* All four of us find a spot just a few rows behind the crowd-control gates, where several photographers with impressive gear are already setting up—the band should be out soon. A few other people are heading back out of the pit, probably eager for a drink now that White Miles has finished. I wrap my arms around Anouk and square my shoulders as much as possible to protect her from the crowd, which is likely to get pretty rowdy tonight.

From the very first song, everyone starts dancing and jumping all around. Nestled in my arms, Anouk tenses up instantly, as predicted. She tries to put on a brave face—*I'm totally fine!*—but I can tell she won't be able to stand it for very long.

"Try to let yourself go with the flow, don't fight it!" I yell loud enough for her to hear, but that just stresses her out more. She's looking around frantically, like a scared puppy. Jessica leans toward her and says something into her ear. Anouk nods, then comes closer to tell me that the three of them are going to head to the back because it's suffocating down here.

Disappointed, I'm about to follow when she motions for me to stay.

"Take advantage of being up so close! Then come find us at the end. Don't worry about it!"

I kiss her on the temple, then watch her leave. Djibril leads them in a single-file line, elbowing his way through the crowd. As they move farther away, the audience swallows them up—everyone's eager to get a few inches closer to the stage.

To my right, a super tall guy bumps into me as he climbs onto a friend's shoulders. He's crowd surfing now, carried overhead by the outstretched arms of the ecstatic audience that's all screaming excitedly or singing the lyrics to the song that's got us swaying in unison. I let myself go and start moshing so hard with those around me that my feet don't even touch the ground anymore.

I figure out that something's wrong when I suddenly fall hard back to the ground. I turn to look at the musicians, as if they can explain what's going on. I expect the singer to tell us in English that they pushed an amp a bit too far, but I get nothing from them. The guitar, the bass, and the drums are all silent—instead there are gunshots and screams. I recognize the sound of bullets, volleys of automatic gunfire, even though it's the first time I've heard them in real life.

Behind me, everyone is struggling to reach the stage, their eyes filled with terror. A girl with her hair in a ballerina bun freezes, then drifts slowly to the floor like a piece of paper dropped gently by the wind. Everything seems to be happening in slow motion. I want to catch her, but her eyes have already gone blank, as if someone pushed her "Off" button.

This isn't a game; it's not pretend. This woman's dead, just feet from me. No one's going to yell, *Cut! A bit less tense next time, please!*

Everyone around me is trying to escape, but all I can do is think of Anouk at the back of the room. I can't just take off and leave her—I have to find her. I push against the crowd, going against the tide, fighting for every step. It feels like every time I manage to gain an inch, I'm quickly pushed back two. The mass of people is as cruel and insurmountable as a tsunami, keeping me from reaching the woman I'm meant to be with.

Then, like reeds in a storm, everyone lies down, throwing themselves to the ground, as if they've just realized that staying upright is the quickest way to earn a bullet in the back of the head. I step over several people before I realize that pretty soon I'll be the only one standing—the perfect target.

So I follow suit. I crouch down, lower my head, and crawl between volleys, which seem to be slowing. Someone next to me murmurs that the shooters are wearing explosive vests. That really clinches my decision to get the hell out of here ASAP. How's there any hope of reasoning with guys who plan to blow themselves up in the end, who aren't even afraid of dying?

I try, from my huddled position, to find Anouk among the people lying on the ground, try to remember what she was wearing, if she had on any bright colors. But there are so many people, so jumbled together and tangled up, that I can't even figure out which legs go with which torsos.

Suddenly, to my right, a group of people stand and run toward what must be an emergency exit. I hesitate, but not for long. Driven by adrenaline, I jump up to escape. I'm not thinking about Anouk anymore, only about saving my own skin, about not dying here like a dog in a ditch.

I run, hoping against hope that I won't be struck by a bullet, trip over someone, or hit a dead end. People are piling up in the narrow hallway that's now like a funnel. Without slowing down, I rush the mass of people, hopping and shoving my way through until I finally manage to get out into the street, where my feet hit the pavement in time to the gunfire, which has started up again behind me.

I keep running and running because there's nowhere to hide, nowhere safe in this street, not even a parked car. I run until I'm out of breath and my lungs are on fire. When my legs slow, I force them to keep moving. The sound of bullets has disappeared, though. I keep walking, convinced they'll catch up with me, that they'll finish me right here in the street. Maybe I'm being irrational, but there's nothing rational about any of this. It would really suck to get shot now.

My heart is pounding so hard in my chest that I'm afraid it'll give out, that it won't be able to handle my mad dash, my fear, my fight for survival. How stupid would it be to die of a heart attack after all that.

I take my cigarettes out of my back pocket, then search for my lighter. Where the hell has the damn thing gone? I check to see if I've maybe left it inside the pack of Marlboros. Just two cigarettes waiting for me.

I have a flash of Anouk lighting one right before posting the photo of the two of us outside the Bataclan on Facebook. She used my jacket to shield us from the wind so the flame wouldn't be blown out right away. I remember thinking she was so clumsy she might burn a hole in the lining of my leather coat.

I quickly dial her number and anxiously count the rings that inevitably lead to her voicemail. "You've reached Anouk. I'm not available right now, but . . ."

Anouk, where are you? Don't tell me you're still in there, that Djibril and Jessica haven't gotten you out.

Djibril and Jessica. I'm about to call them too, then a sudden realization holds me back. If they're still inside, the ringing could get them noticed. A death sentence.

I want to turn around and run back to find Anouk, but my legs won't budge. The truth is that I'm terrified at the very idea of heading back toward that building. The truth is that my feet won't move an inch in that direction. The *truth* is that my life is more important to me than hers, even if I refuse to admit it out loud and try to convince myself that it would be stupid to go back anyway, that I can't do anything for her.

That it's too late to change anything. Too late to save her if she hasn't already saved herself.

10

ROMANE

Everyone's rushing forward, hoping to escape whatever's happening behind us, even though nobody really understands just what that is yet. All I can think is that if everyone else is running, I should run too. If they're trying to escape, there must be a threat.

I grab Adèle's hand and pull her along with me, without saying a word. We follow the crowd, hoping it's the right decision. A guy my little sister's age bumps into me as he heads to the back of the room; I try to push him back the other way. He doesn't get it. I want to yell something at him, grab his sleeve to stop him, but he's already disappeared into all the other unfamiliar faces. I hope he'll realize what a mistake he's making soon and turn around.

Then everyone hits the floor. Adèle and I do the same, still hoping it's the right thing. It doesn't take me long to figure out that the pops echoing relentlessly behind us are gunfire. My instincts are screaming at me to get up and flee, to move as fast as I can, but the lights come on and I remain motionless, like everyone else. I would have preferred to stay in the reassuring darkness, which provided cover and let us believe we could go unnoticed, that we were invisible. The light is blinding, and I suddenly feel so exposed.

My toes are killing me thanks to these stupid too-small cowboy boots. I try to focus on the benign pain in my feet to block out the rest—people going limp just feet from me, puddles of blood turning into streams that tickle my hands.

I want to close my eyes, but not seeing is even more terrifying. I meet the gaze of a guy across from me with light-brown hair, and can't help but be reminded of Gustave Courbet's *Desperate Man* self-portrait. A look of utter despair and incomprehension. I study his face to avoid thinking about anything else: curly wisps of hair on his forehead; a well-tended, very gentlemanly mustache that contrasts with the tousled hairstyle; an aquiline nose; pursed lips gone almost white; a tattoo on his arm of huge purple tentacles slithering down from the sleeve of his T-shirt all the way to his wrist. I count the tentacles as if counting sheep—slowly, carefully. Eight twisting tentacles so perfectly portrayed that they almost seem to be moving, dancing over his skin. I wonder how much of his skin is given over to this octopus. Does its body cover his entire back, does it circle his torso, making him its prisoner?

He doesn't look away, and I wonder if he's staring at me to reassure himself or to comfort me, to let me know I'm not alone. I cling to his gaze for minutes, maybe hours. Nothing seems tangible anymore. Adèle whimpers softly next to me, and I squeeze her hand as hard as I can, not daring to turn my head toward her, not wanting to move even the slightest bit more.

"I can't move my leg anymore, Romane . . . I can't feel my foot!"

Despite my concern, I really just want to tell her to be quiet, not to make even the least bit of noise. Phones are ringing all around us, more and more cells going off, a rush of different melodies and muffled vibrators—so the world outside must *know*?—and I hope against hope that my sister thought to silence hers before the concert started. When I feel mine vibrating against my hip, I push down on it as hard as I can to stifle the sound, so hard my hand starts to cramp.

Don't draw attention, breathe as quietly as possible, don't move despite the unbearable tingling in my legs and the terror spreading through the crowd—invisible, but contagious.

The stranger across from me stands up along with a bunch of other people. He's about to flee, and I pray that he won't be shot before my eyes. He whispers to me to come with him, but I know Adèle wouldn't make it, that she couldn't handle a mad dash right now. I feel like people are playing red light, green light all around us—with every bang, they freeze like statues. As a kid, I was always the first one to reach the wall when I played with my classmates. I was the best. Could I win tonight? Does my life really depend on that stupid game?

I watch him hesitate and look around, then lie back down just as the merciless volleys of gunfire pick up again. Did he stay for my sake? That doesn't make any sense . . .

I dive back into his gaze and convince myself that as long as he's here, everything will be all right. I try to blink as little as possible, only when my eyes are screaming out from the dryness.

He silently mouths something at me, exaggerating his articulation so I can read his lips. *It's going to be okay.* I want to ask him how he can know that, but I simply smile, heartened by this stranger doing his best to make me feel better.

We've been lying here playing dead for hours now. No one's coming to save us. No one's coming, because if they were, they'd already be here.

Or maybe it's only been a few minutes. I don't know anymore.

The gray-eyed man a few yards from me will probably be the last person I ever see. Before heavy footsteps stop in front of me on their hunt for survivors.

I hear them walking around, firing into the crowd as they whisper, "Shh, shh . . . ," almost gently, as if we were children they needed to calm, animals they wanted to reassure before putting them to sleep.

Despite my best efforts otherwise, I can feel hot flashes and cold sweats washing over me in rapid succession. I concentrate on reciting something, anything—it's the only thing that brings me back from the edge once I've started to panic. In my head, I list the ingredients needed to make macarons. I'd taught how to make them at my most recent cooking class, last Sunday. Meanwhile, I keep my eyes fixed on the stranger opposite me, and I decide to call him Charles, to make him seem more familiar. *Charles, let me give you the recipe for macarons. You'll see, they're really not so hard to make, you just have to be patient.* He seems to be listening closely, and for a moment I wonder if telepathy might really work in extreme circumstances like these. *First you sift half a cup of almond flour, to get rid of any clumps. Then you do the same thing with a cup of confectioner's sugar.*

Charles stays focused on me, so I continue. *You whip seven table-spoons of egg whites until they form stiff peaks. I know, it's a pain, and most people would just say three to four egg whites, but macaron-making is an exact science.* I wonder if Charles would really have the patience to measure out the egg whites. He seems more like the kind of guy who'd just use three, thinking it won't make much of a difference. I'll have to ask him later if he'd measure them out or not. *Later . . .*

If we ever stand up and make it out of this concert hall alive, I could actually offer to teach him to make macarons. Having an octopus tattoo doesn't necessarily mean he doesn't like to cook.

When the egg whites are firm, you carefully add one and a half table-spoons of sugar. Charles smiles at me, as if he likes what I'm telling him. My pulse finally starts to slow, and I offer my own shy smile in return.

I keep going with the recipe in my mind, transmitting it to him, without looking away. I ignore the huge explosion that makes me hover off the floor for a split second before my jaw comes crashing back down onto the hard surface. *Pour the almond flour and confectioner's sugar into the egg whites, like snow.* Is the building going to come crashing down, are we going to die here, crushed in the rubble?

Mix it all together as gently as possible—finesse is crucial here. Should I get up? It would be really dumb not to try to escape if everything's about to collapse or explode. Could I carry Adèle, or drag her at least? Would you help me, Charles? *A rubber spatula works best for mixing. The batter should become shiny. You'll know when you've mixed enough.* If the building were going to collapse, it already would have, right? Unless maybe its walls are crumbling slowly, about to give way, taking their time like thunder and lightning—first the flashes of light, then the rumbling, several endless seconds later? *There, that looks perfect. The batter should form a ribbon when you lift the spatula. Chefs actually say it's* macaroning. *Funny word, huh?*

I've used a pastry bag to pipe the macarons onto a cookie sheet, baked them, and even started to prepare the lemon filling, before I finally notice people getting up around me. Adèle sighs deeply in a mixture of relief and pain, and Charles comes over to help me stand her up, as if the two of us have known each other forever.

He quickly figures out that my little sister can't put any weight on her foot, so together we carry her to the exit. It's rather ridiculous, each of us with one arm under Adèle's and the other on our heads, since they asked us to come out with our hands up.

Out in the street, I watch as the EMTs bring out the injured, carrying them on crowd-control barricades used as makeshift gurneys, and I realize we're lucky to be alive.

We're in a crowded building courtyard, and I hear someone behind me ask drily if this is where the after-party's happening. Nobody laughs.

A uniformed woman comes to take care of Adèle. She carefully takes off her ankle boot to assess the injury. There's so much blood that it's clear she'll need to go to the hospital. As I climb into the ambulance with my sister, I look back at Charles and finally ask him his name.

"Léopold," he answers.

When he offers to give me his number, it occurs to me that it's going to be hard to call him anything other than Charles.

"Just in case you want to get together sometime . . . No obligation, though!" he adds almost immediately.

I want to ask him if he likes macarons, but the ambulance doors close before I can reply.

III

After

1

ABIGAËLLE

A few moments later

When her daughter didn't come home after school that evening, Corinne immediately guessed where she'd gone. A quick phone call to Clara's parents confirmed her suspicions.

As usual, her husband suggested that she let it go, not get too worked up about it. "We'll give her a real talking-to when she gets home later. There's no point in ruining *our* evening!"

But—also as usual—she couldn't simply shelve her anger for later. "You do realize this means we have absolutely no authority over her, that she couldn't care less about what we say?"

Her husband sighed and turned off the TV, realizing his plans for a relaxing Friday night had just gone up in a puff of smoke.

Corinne paced the room in circles like a caged lion, furious that her daughter had disobeyed her, that at barely seventeen years old, the girl seemed to have nothing but disregard for her mother. Her anger continued to mount as the hours ticked by. Her husband chose to keep quiet, simply nodding from time to time when the moment seemed right. There was no way he was going to take the brunt of his wife's anger while his daughter enjoyed a concert.

After a while, Abigaëlle's mother finally snatched up her coat and her keys and headed angrily out the door to wait for her daughter outside the concert hall. She figured that it'd be even better if in so doing she managed to humiliate her daughter in front of her friends.

Her husband momentarily thought about trying to dissuade her, but then it occurred to him that if he didn't, he might still get his relaxing evening. As the front door slammed shut behind Corinne, he settled down comfortably in the living room sofa with the TV remote in hand and a slightly guilty smile on his face.

As Corinne climbs the stairs out of the Metro station at ten thirty, the streets of the city's eleventh arrondissement seem awfully noisy, even for a Friday night. All around her, ambulances and police cars are flying past, so she's careful to stay well back on the sidewalk—given the way the night is going, getting run over would be the icing on the cake. The flashing bluish lights leave her with a lingering glare as she walks briskly up Boulevard Voltaire, worried she'll arrive after the end of the concert, miss her daughter, and be left with no outlet for her anger.

When she finds herself facing a wall of police barricades blocking her way, Corinne exasperatedly questions a police officer shouting frantically into his walkie-talkie. He gently pushes her back, motioning for her to turn back.

"You can't stay here, ma'am. It's too dangerous."

"What? What are you talking about? I just want to go pick my daughter up from the Bataclan!"

Looking into the distraught eyes of the uniformed man, Corinne finally realizes something is wrong. She waits for some sort of explanation to come out of the man's mouth, or at least out of the walkie-talkie, which is spitting out snippets of sentences. But when nothing seems forthcoming, she shoves aside one of the barricades and starts forward.

"There's been a mass shooting, ma'am."

Seeing Corinne go pale, clearly unable to grasp what he's just said, the officer continues, "Inside the Bataclan."

She pushes the young man aside with her arm, trying to get past him.

"I'm going to get my daughter."

He holds her back, with a firmness that surprises even him.

"I'm sorry, but you can't go any farther. Have you tried calling her? Hundreds of people have already escaped . . ."

Corinne would like to tell him how many times she's tried to reach her daughter, to explain to him how her anger had mounted as she listened to the phone ring, over and over, until she was filled with a rage that drove her out of her house, drove her to come here with the intent to scream furiously at her carefree daughter who doesn't take anything seriously—especially not her mother.

But all that anger has suddenly turned into fear, into a panic that's dripping down her spine like ice-cold rain. Corinne rifles through her purse to find her phone and dial Abigaëlle's number yet again, in front of the officer, who's clearly uncomfortable. She closes her eyes and holds her breath.

"Hi, you've reached Abi! Can't answer my phone right now, so leave a message!"

"I have to get by, please . . ."

The policeman refuses. Corinne waits. The minutes trudge by slowly, punctuated by muffled gunfire. Every time she hears a new pop of gunfire, she wonders if her daughter's been hit. All she can do is wait. Her powerlessness is torture.

Suddenly her eyes widen at the sound of a huge explosion that sends vibrations running through her legs.

"What was that?"

The officer shakes his head, panicked.

"You can't stay here! You have to go!"

Abigaëlle's mother holds tightly to the barricade, as if to a ship's helm, her eyes focused on the entrance to the Bataclan.

When her husband arrives a few hours later, she hasn't moved. He gently warms her hands, then slowly pulls her tense fingers off the cold metal one by one. He walks her to their car, parked a few streets away, outside the blocked-off area.

"We'll find her. I'm sure she's okay. She must have found a safe place, in a café or at someone's apartment. Clara's mom told me Clara was among the first people to make it out. I'm sure Abigaëlle is safe and sound somewhere."

Corinne doesn't even glance at her husband.

"But where? If she were okay, she would have let us know!"

"Maybe she's lost her phone, or the battery's run out, or . . ."

"Or maybe she's still inside, maybe she's unconscious, or hurt, or even . . ."

Corinne bites her lip, unable to let the thought cross her lips. Her husband can't find any words to comfort her.

They spend the entire night calling police stations and all the hospitals in and around Paris. They position themselves at the town hall of the eleventh arrondissement, and every time a bus rolls up with survivors, they expect to see their daughter trembling in a gold emergency blanket. Every five minutes, Corinne wants to cry, *There she is!* and run over to take some brunette teenage girl in her impatient arms—until she realizes it's not Abigaëlle. It's *never* Abigaëlle.

She falters when she realizes the last bus has arrived and that her daughter isn't on it. In a fit of desperation, she goes so far as to climb inside the bus, checking every row to make sure her daughter's not there, huddled alone on a seat—like when she was six and she'd fallen asleep on the bus during a school outing and her teacher had forgotten about her. In that instance, the driver found her and brought her back to her distraught parents waiting outside the school.

But this time the driver just looks away.

"I'm sorry, ma'am," he mutters, and Corinne wants to explode because she's so tired of hearing that perfectly absurd and useless word.

Her husband is glued to his phone. The answer on the other end is always the same: "We don't know." Nobody knows anything. Everyone is overwhelmed. And their daughter is still missing.

He keeps repeating the same thing over and over again in his head, to keep from panicking or falling to pieces. *As long as she's missing, she's not dead. As long as she's missing, she's not dead. As long as she's missing . . .*

Saturday morning seems to go on forever, every minute drawn out in an unbearable waiting game marked by a mix of hope and primal fear that they will never find their child. One of the hospitals asks if their daughter has any kind of distinctive marking—a tattoo, a scar—but there's nothing on Abigaëlle's body that would make it easy to identify her at a glance. They ask what she was wearing, but her parents have no idea. They'd barely seen her that morning before she left for school. On the phone, Clara sobs as she tells them about the turquoise tights, but that detail seems pretty small and pointless.

"I can't even tell them what my daughter was wearing last night! Brown hair and blue tights, that's all she is now! So we're sitting by our phones, both hoping for and dreading a ring, helpless . . . We can't do a damn thing, and it's driving me crazy!"

Her disconcerted husband nods gently, just like he did the night before.

◆ ◆ ◆

Back home, late that afternoon, Corinne's phone vibrates on the kitchen table, and she jumps up to answer, bumping into an open cabinet door on the way.

"Hello?"

"Hello, ma'am, I'm calling from Pompidou Hospital. Your daughter Abigaëlle is here, in the post-operative recovery room."

Corinne is silent, unable to believe what she's hearing. Maybe she's imagining the conversation, like she imagined seeing her daughter dozens of times last night.

"She was shot twice, in her lower back and thigh, but the operation went well. The surgeon will explain everything face-to-face . . ."

The tears finally start rolling, without a sound.

"Ma'am? Can you hear me? Hello?"

Corinne swallows the lump in her throat and takes in a sharp breath of air, just enough to whisper, "We're on our way."

When they finally arrive outside room 223, Corinne lets her husband go in first. She takes a second to steady herself and quiet her fears.

Abigaëlle seems so small, lying there on the big white bed amid IV lines and beeping machines. Her daughter opens her eyes with difficulty and offers a small smile.

Wordlessly, her mother walks over and clasps the teenager's hand in her own.

"I thought we'd never find you . . . ," she whispers before bursting into tears.

Abigaëlle squeezes her mother's hand to get her attention, and Corinne strokes her daughter's face.

"You know what I was thinking, Mom?"

Her mother shakes her head, wiping tears from her cheeks.

"If you'd let me dye my hair red, you would've found me faster, you know!"

Corinne perches on the side of the bed and clumsily bumps her daughter's leg. Abigaëlle doesn't react, as if she hasn't felt it. Her mother furrows her brow, but says nothing, preoccupied.

"We'll talk about that later, okay?"

Reassured, Abigaëlle closes her eyes, leaving her hand in her mother's.

2

Philippe

An hour later

He doesn't know how much time they spent like that, lying with their noses pressed flat against the floor, their faces crying out in pain, arms and legs totally asleep. An hour? Two, three? Pascal feels like it lasted for days, but at the same time like it went by in a flash. It's hard to explain; it was as if time no longer existed, like in a nightmare, when it feels like it's been going on forever, but in reality it's only been a few seconds.

He closed his eyes to keep from seeing, to try to block everything out, to forget. Philippe's voice soothed him for a long time—he held on to it like a lifeboat. His friend kept talking, kept reassuring him, and Pascal chose to believe him, to trust him when he said it'd all be over soon.

And then Philippe stopped whispering in his ear. Probably because he'd gone through his stock of comforting words. The two men stayed there, still and silent, plastered to the floor.

Pascal didn't even budge when a huge explosion shook the whole building. He crossed his fingers that the ceiling wouldn't come tumbling down on them—that would have been a shitty way to go. But the walls held, and so did he and Philippe.

He only dared open his eyes when a cop told them to get up and head outside. He felt others hurrying to stand, wobbling, but he preferred to wait until the navy-blue uniform came into view, to make sure it wasn't the shooters tricking those who'd only been playing dead into showing themselves. There was no way he'd fall for that, not after waiting for so long already.

Philippe didn't say anything, and that surprised him, because he's used to Philippe making the decisions. What to do, what game, concert, or bar to go to, what day and time. Pascal likes following his lead.

But Pascal had to move after a while. He heard people yelling for help, people who were wounded and couldn't walk out on their own. He wriggled out from under Philippe and to his knees, then shook his friend.

"Let's get the hell out of here! C'mon, let's go!"

He shook him again, but his friend didn't move. It took all his strength to turn Philippe onto his back. He's a big guy—at least two hundred pounds. That's when Pascal saw the red stain on his friend's beige sweater, on his chest.

"Philippe, wake up!" he urged. "Wake up, damn it! We have to go!"

He slapped his friend's cheeks while putting pressure on his torso— he'd taken a first-aid class last year through work, just before getting laid off.

And then he panicked.

He refused to understand, because it was all so unbelievable.

People passed by him, eager to reach the nearest exit, to make it out into the street and take a deep breath of the cold November air. But Pascal felt like all the oxygen in the room had been sucked out in a single second.

He was suffocating, choking. He took his unmoving friend in his arms and screamed, begged someone to come help them. The silence had protected them for so long, but now he wanted everyone to hear him. His voice was unrecognizable, distorted by fear and anguish.

A police officer took Philippe's pulse, then shook his head sorrowfully. "It's over, I'm sorry. You can't stay here. I'll escort you out."

No way was he was going to abandon his friend in that room, alone in a puddle of blood.

"I won't leave him."

"There's nothing more to be done. You really have to go . . ."

Pascal was dazed, acting as if on autopilot.

"I won't leave him," he said again, more firmly. But the officer explained that he had to take care of the wounded first, that he couldn't leave him sitting there.

So Pascal stood and tried to carry Philippe. Impossible. He started dragging him, hands under Philippe's arms, leaving a bright-red trail on the floor. The policeman watched him without saying a word. Pascal could see that the officer felt just as lost as he did.

Then all of a sudden his strength abandoned him. He saw himself for the poor idiot he was, trying to drag his dead buddy out of there. He let go and stood up straight, but then had no idea what to do next. His head was spinning and there was nothing to grab hold of. The police officer helped him move slowly toward the main entrance to the Bataclan—or what was now the exit.

"You're lucky, you know," the cop muttered. "Whatever you do, don't look around."

Of course Pascal looked around after that—he couldn't help it. Bodies, flesh, sticky puddles of blood. He couldn't even see the floor through the human wreckage. But that didn't make him feel any worse than he already did. Philippe was dead and that made enough grief to fill his whole body—there was no room left for any others.

The young officer led him to a courtyard stuffed full of people and left him there, propped against a wall. Pascal slid down toward the ground until he was seated, knees pressed against his chin.

He doesn't know how long he stayed in that cobblestone court-yard, with everyone's adrenaline still pumping, though the threat had vanished. He was examined, offered orange juice and coffee, wrapped in an emergency blanket. People asked if they could get him anything, if he wanted to talk, but he had no words. The din made him wish he still had his earplugs to block everyone out, to cut himself off from the world.

It all just seemed so absurd. He'd let Philippe die, lying on top of him. He'd been listening to the sound of his voice, but didn't even worry when it suddenly went silent. His friend had protected him that whole time, and Pascal didn't even realize he'd been shot, that Philippe was bleeding out as he soothed him. He didn't even feel his old friend's blood on his back or his body getting heavier. Pascal never tried to comfort Philippe, or answer his whispers. He'd only thought about himself, about his own survival. Philippe died a hero—but for what? For a loser who could never have done as much, who even now can't manage get off his ass to help the people suffering mere feet away from him.

All of a sudden, he thinks of his friend's wife and children, of the fact that he's going to have to explain why he's coming home alone. Why he survived, but Philippe did not. How he was cowardly and his friend brave. How he was selfish, while Philippe was generous, as always, even until the very end. Pascal wants to run far, far away to avoid that moment. He regrets not dying in Philippe's place, or at least by his side. He glances at his phone and realizes people are worried about them, that they want to be reassured as soon as possible, so they keep calling, again and again.

He finally works up the courage to stand, though he isn't too steady. He carefully places the shiny emergency blanket on the ground—it can still be of use to someone else, no reason to waste it. Ignoring the EMTs, he quickly crosses the courtyard. No one stops him, so he continues into the street. For a long time, he walks determinedly, like a robot, head down, heavy with guilt, until he reaches the sky-blue Renault Scénic they drove to the concert. He walks around to wait on the passenger side of the car before finally realizing that Philippe isn't there to drive, and that he obviously doesn't have his friend's keys.

Pascal finally starts to cry, his back pressed against the cold metal of the locked car, alone in the dark Parisian night.

3

Sofiane

A day later

Sofiane came home late that night, in a daze. Héloïse was ready to pounce, to throw wedding favors in his face, to bombard him with the tiny white and silver candies as punishment for leaving her to work on the little heart-shaped construction-paper envelopes alone for hours.

But when she finally heard the key in the lock and he opened the door, she saw the look on his face and realized something was wrong. She walked over to her fiancé, and he threw himself into her arms, almost ferociously. His hands were freezing, and he seemed chilled to the bone.

After a few minutes, she peppered him with questions. Had something bad happened, had he been mugged, had he gotten some terrible news? Sofiane opened his mouth, but not a single sound crossed his lips. So he turned on the TV, and Héloïse thought that he had a hell of a lot of nerve to start watching without saying even a single word to explain himself.

She kept staring at her fiancé while he stared at the screen, seemingly hypnotized by the whirlwind of dark images flashing by. Héloïse finally followed his gaze, instinctively.

That's when she understood. She dropped down onto the couch next to him as the video montage, which had been broadcasting on a continuous loop for some time at that point, streamed across the screen. They watched together, both eager for more and devastated at the sight.

Wordlessly, she took his hand and squeezed hard. She wrapped her arms around him and pressed his head to her chest, awkwardly stroking his hair. Sofiane focused on the muffled sound of Héloïse's heart pounding inside her rib cage.

As they watched the stretchers cross the screen again and again, Héloïse had an indescribable feeling that their lives could have taken an irreversible turn on that unseasonably warm fall night.

They went to bed, where she soothed her future husband like a newborn, whispering softly to him and rocking him almost imperceptibly against her body. Sofiane finally fell asleep, exhausted, but the rest of the night was regularly interrupted by nightmares, from which he woke screaming and drenched in sweat. The faintest sound of a siren outside made him tremble, and a car door slamming made him jump. He imagined he could hear footsteps coming from behind their bedroom door, so Héloïse opened it to show him no one was there. But he could still hear them—behind the walls, or at the front door, or in the stairwell. Footsteps coming and going without stopping, looking for him, hunting him.

Usually, when you settle into bed after a concert, it's the music you keep hearing, like an echo. But Sofiane was possessed by the sound of those heavy, inescapable, fatal footsteps.

A terrible thought occurred to Héloïse: even though her fiancé had come home alive, he may not have made it out unscathed. Part of him might have been left behind at the Bataclan, at the bottom of the aptly named pit. The memories and flashbacks that were now a part of him might traumatize him and change him forever. This ordeal might slowly distance him from her—because he would never really be able to *share* his fear and anxiety with her.

As the morning light begins to shine shyly behind the opaque curtains in their room, the couple sit up in bed, relieved that the horrific night is finally over. Their features are drawn and their faces pale.

Héloïse hurries into the kitchen to make breakfast. Sofiane's telephone vibrates on the nightstand, and he jumps up in a panic. The slightest noise terrifies him, though he tries to pretend he's all right. His fiancée notices, and even though she doesn't really understand his exaggerated reactions, even though she knows she'll never really understand them, she does her best to keep quiet. She doesn't use the Nespresso machine because of the loud buzzing sound it makes as the coffee flows. Instead she rifles through the back of the cabinet to find an old drip coffee maker that hasn't been used in several years; it doesn't make such a racket.

While the coffee is brewing, she sits down next to Sofiane, who's lain back in bed, a pillow clutched between his arms. He's looking out the window, lost in thought.

"What do you want to do today?"

"Forget," he blurts immediately.

Héloïse can feel the lump in her throat growing. She wishes she could take away his fear and pain, or even wipe his memory clean. She suddenly feels utterly powerless.

"We could go for a walk in the woods? Or for a bike ride?"

Her words seem so frivolous when compared with what's going on in Sofiane's head.

"They said on the news that there's a psychological support team. I could go with you, if you want to talk to someone. I'm sure it would do you good to talk it through . . ."

Sofiane shakes his head listlessly.

"I don't want to go out. Or talk. I just want to wait for it to go away. Would you mind if we stayed home today?"

"Of course not."

Héloïse gets the coffee. As she's leaving the kitchen with two steaming mugs, she realizes her fiancé has moved to the living room, where he's sitting in front of the news, still broadcasting the same images from the night before on an endless loop.

She's not sure it's a good idea to let him dwell on the footage, or if she should try to get him to think about something else—or if she even could. She slowly extends one of the mugs to Sofiane, who grabs it without taking his eyes off the screen.

The phone keeps ringing, all day long—calls from close friends, mere acquaintances, family, and colleagues. Héloïse listens as Sofiane parrots the same couple of sentences over and over, in an affectedly cheerful voice: "Friday the thirteenth brought me good luck for once! I never win a dime from the lottery, never win any game, but this time, luck was on my side . . ." He laughs with whoever's on the line, plays up the dark humor, saying he wonders if his ticket will be reimbursed, but as soon as he hangs up, his eyes go blank again—all the pretending seems to take a toll on him.

He's glued to his cell phone, following the news on Twitter, contemplating the photos of every victim and every missing person. Héloïse suspects he's running through the night in his head, trying to decide if he saw the young blonde woman or spoke to the bearded guy, if he knows anything that could help, anything that could be useful. He studies the portraits one after another, without saying a word, and she doesn't dare ask what he's thinking.

She's fairly certain that he's in shock, from waiting, terrified, in the makeshift attic, and from everything else he saw last night, but she doesn't know what she's supposed to do or say. Maybe just being there for him is enough; maybe she simply needs to let him get his bearings.

As the sun is setting, he finally looks at her and asks, distraught, "What in the world am I going to tell my students? How am I going to be able to explain all this to a class of seven-year-olds?"

At first, Héloïse doesn't know what to say. She tries to put herself in a teacher's shoes, in the shoes of the children, who are still so naïve and full of hope.

"I'm not sure you can really 'explain' anything . . . There's no answer to the question *why* . . ."

"But they're going to ask. They'll want to understand. I know them, they'll never let it go if they feel like it's not totally clear . . ."

"Then deflect the questions you can't answer into subjects you *can* talk about. All you can do is tell them not to be scared, that there's no reason to be. Talk to them about the music . . ."

4

BASTIEN

Two days later

For the first time in years, René closed his butcher shop on a Sunday. Market day.

He left the metal security shutter down, without even bothering to put up a sign explaining his absence. Around nine o'clock, his usual customers started showing up outside the silent storefront, where they agreed that closing on a Sunday morning really wasn't very businesslike.

The day before, he'd gone to work like he had every other day, because there was no way he could sit idly by, watching the news. As long as they didn't know anything, the best thing to do was to go about business as usual. Fear does not keep danger at bay, as René's father had always said.

So when he'd gotten the call, he'd been busy wrapping up a four-pound roast for a tight-lipped elderly woman. The phone had rung several times in a row, so he'd finally decided to answer it, despite the long line of customers in a hurry to get through their weekend errands, despite the choir of dissatisfied sounds they had made when he had headed to the cold room for some privacy.

He had nodded and mumbled hesitantly, "Yes, I understand. I'll work something out . . ." Then he'd gently put his phone down on the counter and gone back to his customers. He'd kept working for hours, like a robot. Slicing, weighing, wrapping. He couldn't bring himself to call his wife, because he knew firsthand that hope was better than utter emptiness and despair.

Then, today, earlier in the afternoon, after dragging his feet getting ready and handing tissue after tissue to his wife, he got in his car and headed for the capital. Without really thinking about it, he chose to take backroads rather than the main A13 highway, to avoid getting there too quickly. He was in no hurry, and anything that would postpone his arrival was welcome.

It hadn't been too hard to persuade his wife to stay at home with her sister, who'd come from Le Havre when she'd heard the news. His wife couldn't have come anyway—she could barely stand; she was as limp as a dead leaf. For almost a day now, she'd only been able to repeat one thing, over and over, saying it so many times that the words had lost all meaning: "I bought him the ticket. It's my fault, it's all my fault . . ." René knew he should have told her she was wrong, that he should have comforted her, told her she had nothing to do with it, that there was no reason to hold herself accountable. He knew all that, but God was it hard to console someone else when he felt like he was falling apart himself. His sister-in-law had taken over, spoken the soothing words in his stead. He had no idea that, to his wife, his silence was full of accusation and blame, a conviction with no chance of appeal.

Before he left for Paris, she'd given him a votive candle in a glass yogurt jar—"to protect the flame and keep it burning"—and made him promise to place it alongside all the other wavering lights and bouquets she'd seen placed in homage at Place de la République. A terribly feeble defense against bullets and grief.

When he arrives at the orange-brick building that houses the coroner's office, his legs suddenly stop, and René fears that despite his brain's urging, they may refuse to go any farther. He can't remember exactly what they'd told him on the phone yesterday. He was shaken, and now everything seems so jumbled in his head. He had wanted to call back to ask if he had to come, but didn't dare. The hoarse voice on the other end of the line had told him they were sure. They'd found Bastien's wallet on him, with his ID inside. The T-shaped scar right under his left eyebrow meant there wasn't a shadow of a doubt: it was him. René still remembered his son running around the grocery store that morning, not listening, how he'd rammed headfirst into a cart steered by a young woman in a hurry to finish her shopping. There had been blood everywhere, and she had screamed, but hadn't dared touch the little boy, who'd been too dazed to cry. René had picked Bastien up matter-of-factly and energetically dabbed at the wound with his checkered handkerchief. In the end, they'd gone to the emergency room for two stitches. He never took Bastien grocery shopping again.

The chain-smoking woman's voice had also mentioned the four hoops in his son's left ear, and that's when René's heart skipped a beat. Who else would have had the crazy idea to decorate their ear like a goddamn Christmas tree?

No, there was no room for doubt, no place for hope to hide. René didn't know if identifying the body was mandatory, or if they had simply offered him the chance to see his son one last time. So he could come to terms with reality, see it with his own eyes.

◆ ◆ ◆

And here, now, in front of the empty stairs leading up to the building, seemingly waiting for him alone, he has no desire, no need to see his child's body riddled with bullets, even though he's been reassured—as if it were any consolation—that his face was spared.

Without thinking, he reaches out and places his right hand on one of the stone columns that flank the entrance to the morgue, to catch his breath and work up the courage. A graying man who looks about fifty comes over and asks quietly—the situation seems to call for silence—if he is all right. René nods and gestures for the stranger to continue on his way. The man doesn't press him further.

As he enters the building and walks slowly through the main hall, the childless father hopes the body he's about to see won't irreversibly replace all the other memories he has of his little boy, all the vibrant images that pop spontaneously into his head when he thinks of Bastien. The way he squished his eyes shut with all his strength when blowing out his birthday candles as a kid, only opening them once his lungs were totally empty, eager to see if he'd managed to put them all out at once. *That means my wish will come true, Daddy!* he would say, delighted with his accomplishment, and René would nod. *Yes, I'm sure it will, Bastien.* His obsession with picking all sorts of insignificant objects up off the ground: rocks, half-rusted paperclips, pieces of string. *I'm going to keep it. It's my treasure!* he would announce, indifferent to his father's admonitions, *I don't want trash all over the house!* The day when he called to tell his parents that he'd finished among the top ten students in his graduating glass. René can still hear his casual tone, the way he wasn't surprised at all. Bastien's success had always been a given. When he hung up, he saw his wife's tears of joy and shook his head before heading out to mow the lawn, which had been in need of attention for a while. Once hidden from view and enveloped in the buzzing of the mower's motor, he wiped a tear from his cheek, his heart suddenly swollen with pride at the thought of the amazing future that awaited his son.

◆ ◆ ◆

When he finally climbs back down the steps and finds himself overlooking the Seine, it's dusk. René, who's only been to Paris a handful of times, gets out his map of the city and looks for Place de la République. The glass yogurt container in his coat pocket jingles against his belt buckle whenever he moves.

After a few minutes, he concludes that it shouldn't take more than a half hour to walk there, and decides to leave his car where it is. He flips his coat collar up and pushes forward into the capital's deserted streets, taking deep breaths of cold air until his lungs ache.

The statue of Marianne, a symbol of the French Revolution and an allegory of liberty and democracy, is surrounded, overrun with flowers still in their plastic wrapping, and little orange flames. René had naïvely thought he'd be alone to grieve and pay tribute, but there are hundreds, maybe even thousands of other people there. He sees the police armed to the teeth and thinks sadly that they're a bit late. He hears voices shouting, "We're not afraid!" and wants to say there's no reason to be afraid now—the worst has already happened.

He studies the scene before him, which is quickly becoming a memorial: white roses; drawings in plastic sleeves to protect them from the rain that's bound to come soon; the blue, white, and red striped flags; brightly colored wreaths; the candleholders, which are starting to pile up; and the kneeling people carefully relighting the candles that have gone out. René patiently waits his turn. He doesn't want to elbow his way to the front—he's in no hurry.

Suddenly he's jostled by the crowd. All around him, people are screaming, running. Fleeing. René takes advantage of the situation to get closer to the statue, where he stands unmoving, watching men and women stampeding like animals, trampling each other and groaning in terror. "We're not afraid!" *Yeah right,* thinks Bastien's father. Without knowing what's caused the tumult, he observes as people take refuge in cafés that are already bursting at the seams, while others fan out to neighboring streets. He watches them scurry away like rabbits, unable to feel anything himself, caught in a stupor. He doesn't even wonder why they're running away; he doesn't really care. The only question in his mind is whether his son also tried to escape. Did he run like that too?

Maybe those were gunshots that just rang out. Could be. But René isn't paying attention to the noises around him. A building could collapse a few yards away without his heart jumping into his throat. He doesn't have the energy or the drive to run anyway. What's the point now? He wasn't able to admit to his son that he loved him unconditionally before it was too late. Now all he'll have left is regrets, filtering into his heart like a slow poison.

René despondently takes the yogurt jar and the tiny white candle from his coat pocket. He lights it, doing his best to protect it from the freezing gusts of wind, then gently places it next to a peace sign drawn in black ink. As the trembling flame warms the small glass, he drops in four silver hoops one by one, then turns and leaves without looking back.

5

Léopold

A week later

Romane had copied Léopold's number down on the white board in her kitchen before the ink faded from her palm. In case she wanted to give him a shot, as he'd mumbled with a smile before she left with Adèle for the hospital. At the time, she'd found the expression particularly awkward, and she'd seen in Léopold's eyes that he was thinking the same thing.

At the end of the weekend, Adèle, whose foot had actually only been grazed by fragments, had hurried home to their native Dijon on crutches, eager to get back to their roommates and be pampered by their parents, who lived just a few streets away. Though it was hard, Romane had gone back to work at the Ministry the following Monday, as the phone calls from friends and family gradually slowed, leaving behind a devastating solitude, a loneliness so intense that she felt like she was drowning.

Then, the following Friday night, it all suddenly became intolerable as she watched the clock hands tick closer to nine thirty. She picked up the phone and dialed Léopold's number.

She had no idea what she was going to say, so when he picked up, she felt incredibly stupid, muttering, "It's Romane," in a voice that was slightly too shrill. There was a pretty good chance he wouldn't even remember her name—so much had happened that night.

But Léopold knew who she was right away. They went through the usual small talk, both of them self-consciously not asking the other how he or she was doing. They talked about the weather getting colder, about Adèle heading home, about Léopold's three friends, who were all safe and sound. Léopold really understood what she was going through, could hear the distress, sadness, and fear in her voice, maybe because he'd been wrestling with the same strange feelings himself for the past week.

Before hanging up, they made plans to have lunch together the next day, in a bistro near the Jardin des Plantes. Romane hadn't dared admit to Léopold that even the idea of going to a restaurant terrified her, and Léopold hadn't bothered her with the fact that he lived in Amiens, because the two-hour drive to and from the capital to see Romane again didn't bother him one bit.

When they walk into the restaurant on Saturday, they make sure to ask the waiter for the table located the farthest from the door and windows. Better safe than sorry.

And now that she's across from him, now that he can enjoy the sweet way she brushes her long bangs out of her eyes, Léopold asks the question he couldn't bring himself to ask on the phone.

"How are you?"

Romane tries to go off on a tangent, to sidestep the question altogether, but he cuts her off in the kindest way possible, and repeats, "How are you?"

And for the first time, she doesn't say she's doing all right. She doesn't try to "put things into perspective," or reassure the person asking the question, like she has with her sister, her parents, her friends, and her coworkers. She doesn't try to fool him. With her elbows on the table and her head in her hands, she confides in Léopold as if they've known each other forever, feeling like he's the only one she can talk to who really understands—and it's true.

She tells him about Adèle, who seems just as carefree as ever, as if nothing could ever get her down. She tells him about her nightmares and leaving the lamp on her bedside table turned on all night long. She tells him that she has to take Atarax to sleep, and how guilty she feels about being in such a state when she's lucky to simply be alive. She tells him how alone she feels, how it seems like she's walked through a door, leaving everyone else behind in a different world, where everything from her life before is like a scene out of movie or a dream. She tells him how in meetings her brain suddenly loses its ability to focus, carried away by waves of horrific visions that keep coming back. She tells him that she can't take the Metro anymore because of the groaning tracks, and that she's always discreetly looking for the emergency exit wherever she goes. She describes the memory that haunts her, of the exact moment when it all went to hell, that fraction of a second when the world turned upside down. She tells him about the unshakable feeling she has that it was all fake, that she imagined everything that happened that night, and how ever since it's seemed like she's floating above the rest of the world, like she has no place in it anymore. She tells him how everything else now seems so silly and superficial: grocery shopping, cleaning her apartment, going to the pharmacy for throat lozenges, being jostled in the street by rushed passersby. She tells him how afraid she is that *it* will never go away, that it will be a part of her forever, that it will swallow her up, devour her before she can work up the strength to fight back.

Léopold listens without saying a word. He clenches his jaw and, despite his best efforts, his eyes tear up. Because though he's a bit better at holding his demons at bay, every single word that comes out of Romane's mouth could be his. He understands everything she's feeling, emotions that others can't even imagine. Of course he'd like to comfort her and tell her that they'll pass, that they'll fade. But the truth is that he has no idea, even if the psychiatrist he's been seeing has told him that all these emotions are perfectly normal. He sits there, powerless, only managing to place his hand on Romane's, eliciting a smile from her teary face.

When it's his turn to speak, he talks about other things. He tells her about the concert he, Sylvain, Tiago, and Alexandre put on last Saturday night, after spending the entire day at the hotel wondering whether or not it was a good idea to go on stage, wondering if they even could, if the audience would dare venture out to a café for the evening. He tells her what a stressful decision it was, how they felt like having a good time would be inappropriate, almost indecent, and describes the café owner's face when the band showed up with their instruments. He tells her how beat-up the drum set he had to use was, that it must have seen its fair share of more or less gifted drummers before him. He tells her how he managed to keep tempo when they played "Territorial Pissings," and he doesn't even mind that she just shakes her head without understanding what a major accomplishment that was. He tells her about their music, and how it brings him back to life.

When she finally admits that she hasn't been able to listen to any music for the past week, not a single song, he's shocked. Even more than by anything else she's confided in him.

"So I guess if I ask you to listen to one of our latest compositions, you'll refuse?"

Romane shakes her head hesitantly.

Léopold pulls out some earbuds and plugs them into his phone. After tapping at the screen briefly, he hands them to the young woman, who doesn't dare say no. She pushes them into her ears, without looking away from Léopold, using his eyes like a buoy, like she did that night.

A gravelly male voice starts singing very softly, then the instruments burst onto the track one by one. First the guitar, then the bass, which lays out the choppy rhythm, then finally the drums. Romane squeezes Léopold's hand and lets the music fill her head.

She forgets the sound of glasses clinking at the bar, forgets the loud laughter of the group at the table a few feet away, forgets the door to the restaurant, slamming open and shut every time someone comes in or out, forgets the motorcycles buzzing in the streets, buses hurtling over clanging sewer grates, and jack hammers pounding away in the distance.

She listens to the music, paying special attention to the drums, and she forgets.

6

Margot

Two weeks later

She was the only one in the family who had agreed to attend. The organizers had kindly offered to pay for a taxi all the way from Nantes, to make things easier for her. At eighty-four years old, and with a bad hip, Margot's grandmother, Michelle, wouldn't have been able to take the train on her own and navigate the unfamiliar stations and streets.

Margot's parents were so consumed by anger and resentment at the senseless way they'd lost their daughter and son-in-law that they'd refused to attend, and William's parents were simply too sick with grief. And who could blame them? They had their hands full with Sacha. Their grandson was still babbling, smiling, and demanding all the attention the world could offer—he kept them going, kept them grounded in day-to-day life. They had no choice. So Michelle had decided it was up to her to represent her granddaughter and her husband at the memorial service in Paris. Someone had to be there; she couldn't bear it otherwise.

They sat her in the front row, because climbing the bleacher stairs would have been too complicated with her cane. Everyone pampered her, but their good will was powerless to warm her soul, especially in this huge cobblestone courtyard, where even the slightest gust of freezing air managed to find its way past her pilly wool coat.

The seats filled one by one, but Michelle stayed focused on the black-uniformed band that kept playing pieces she didn't know. She still had so many unanswered questions, and not knowing, having no one to answer them, was suffocating her.

Had Margot suffered, had she screamed in pain, had William been there to hold her in his arms until the end, had they had time to tell each other good-bye? Had she been caught by surprise; had her life simply been extinguished in a split second, before she realized what was going on, or had she tried to escape, her eyes wide with terror? Had she suffered for hours? Had she been scared, had someone stayed with her to reassure and comfort her? Had she been excited about the concert, had she been looking forward to going on a date with her husband for weeks? Had she felt the bullets wedge deep in her flesh, had she watched the dark-red stain spread on the fabric of her dress without understanding where it was coming from? Had her granddaughter even been wearing a dress that night? Had she helped other people get out of that cursed building, or had she thought only of saving herself, even if that meant trampling the wounded without remorse?

For the past two weeks, Michelle has been trying desperately to quiet these incessant questions. In vain. She keeps them to herself, though, forming a lump in her throat, because she doesn't want to upset her daughter any more than she already is. And nobody has the answers anyway.

She told herself she could share her grief with others by coming here, but when she finally finds herself sitting in an uncomfortable chair amid a sea of strange, solemn faces, she realizes just how solitary mourning really is.

◆ ◆ ◆

The din quiets when the president arrives and "La Marseillaise" is played—a bit too enthusiastically for Margot's grandmother, who would prefer gentle, soothing music.

She watches as he sits stoically in a lone chair across from the bleachers, and she feels a bit sorry for him, up there all by himself. She wishes she could pull her chair up next to him so he doesn't have to be alone, carrying the weight of this terrible massacre on his shoulders.

Three young women sing Jacques Brel's "Quand on n'a que l'amour," and Michelle has flashes of Sunday mornings at home years ago, when Henri would turn on the record player. She sees Margot and her cousins dancing and spinning around their grandfather's legs as he tries to push them aside, in a hurry to get back to whatever he's working on in his little office. She can hear her deceased husband's grouchy voice, but especially the little girls' squeals of delight.

My dress spins the best, doesn't it, Grandma? Margot would ask pleadingly.

Yes, my love, your dress spins the best . . .

Michelle wraps her coat tight around herself, and it occurs to her that Jacques Brel is ruined for her now. She studies the three young women, who look about the same age as the granddaughter she's lost, and she can feel her heart tightening in her rib cage, like a sponge being wrung out, squeezing out every last drop, every last tear. She shivers as she listens—from sadness, grief, and the cold. On a screen to her right, photos of the victims flash by in sets of five. Michelle forces herself not to look; she doesn't want to see the smiling, carefree faces, like those of Margot and William. She stares straight down, focusing on the pale-gray cobblestones, to avoid catching a glimpse of her granddaughter on the screen.

When a blonde woman starts singing "Perlimpinpin" by Barbara, Michelle whispers the words along with her, softly, just for herself. And for Margot—though she probably wouldn't have liked the song. *It's too slow, Grandma! You can't dance to it, and music is meant for dancing!* Her granddaughter had tried quite a few times to get her to listen to modern music, to strange bands that seemed to yell more than they sang. Wild music, as her Henri used to say. And yet, it occurs to Michelle that it's rather strange to memorialize all these young people who listened to rock music by singing "La Marseillaise" and Barbara. She wonders if Margot and William would have appreciated the lyric tone, the solemn, weighty atmosphere.

A man and a woman begin listing all the names of the victims and their ages. Slowly, clearly. It's never-ending. Michelle suddenly feels empty—her granddaughter and son-in-law are just two names amid so many others, and she's just another grieving grandmother among so many other broken families.

But it seems so clear to her that Margot was unique. There are so many things her grandmother could say about her. If she'd been here today, she would have spent her time moaning about the cold, because she would have forgotten her scarf or her gloves—she always forgot something. She would have struck up a conversation with the person sitting next to her as if they were old friends, because that's how she was: engaging and talkative. She would have had tears streaming down her face, and she would have worn them proudly, without a trace of embarrassment, wiping them away with the back of her hand when they itched, and sniffling, because she never tried to hide her emotions. And because, obviously, she would have forgotten to bring tissues.

But if Margot had been here today, there would have been no today at all.

A cello starts playing, a tormented cry that suddenly fills the courtyard of Les Invalides. It makes Michelle want to get up and leave, taking her unspeakable grief with her. She doesn't know why she came anymore, why she thought this ceremony would help her find some peace, why she thought being surrounded by people who are suffering as much as she is would lessen her own pain. Grieving alongside all of France doesn't make her feel better; the fact that Margot and her husband belong to the entire country in a way, that they've become symbols, anonymous celebrities whose names are on everyone's lips, doesn't comfort her in the least. The cello stabs at her heart, slicing deep as it brings back memories of her granddaughter. The bow seems to be playing directly on her nerves, and Michelle has to fight the sudden urge to double over, bested by two invisible hands doing their utmost to twist her esophagus into knots.

Then the president stands up, crosses the courtyard with measured steps, and begins to speak in a somber tone. Michelle thinks of the people listening to him on their television screens, busy with other things in the warmth of their own homes.

Tonight she'll be back in her home, a house too big for her and her orange cat. She'll sit back in her easy chair with the lever for adjusting the back, and the big tomcat will purr on her lap, pleased to have his owner back. Michelle will look through the old photo albums one more time, watching her granddaughter grow up as she turns the pages—her first smile, first steps, first pair of glasses. Her birthdays. Waving at the camera in her white wedding dress. Lovingly kissing her little Sacha at the maternity ward.

She'll look at the pictures again and again, hoping that somehow, if she just keeps doing it, her heart will go numb and the grief will fade.

7

Daphné

A month later

Eight-year-old Charline hasn't been able to get much of an explanation out of her parents, but from what's been said at school—and especially on the playground—she's managed to piece together what happened on the night of November 13.

She wishes she could ask her mother about it more, but Daphné refuses to talk about what she saw. Charline imagines all sorts of things instead.

Despite that, she's been reassured to see her mother looking happy and energetic for the past month. "She's living life to the fullest," as her father says. And everyone is thrilled with the new Daphné, who takes her time rather than rushing around and worrying herself sick about every little thing.

She's still often late picking Charline up at school, but it doesn't seem to upset her anymore. She just offers the principal a big smile and wishes her a wonderful evening, and Mrs. Coullet does the same, surprised to discover how contagious a mother's good mood can be.

Daphné enjoys cooking on the weekend now too. She no longer sees it as a chore, and Charline is thrilled to help her prepare lentil-and-sausage stew and moussaka.

All the little things in life that used to stress Daphné out are now a source of enjoyment. So while Charline's head is still full of unanswered questions she wishes she could ask, she doesn't want her mother to think any negative thoughts, especially since she's afraid that at any minute Daphné might start running around trying to beat the clock again.

Sometimes she notices her mother staring into space, her eyes empty, unseeing. Other times she freezes in the middle of talking or doing something. Sometimes Charline has to repeat, "It's your turn!" insistently, when they're playing board games together. And she occasionally forgets to close her bedroom door at night, or turn off the stair light. A few days ago, Daphné even left the water running in the bathroom. When Charline realized it, she simply went and turned it off, without mentioning it, because she really doesn't want to worry anyone.

She knows her mother's mind wanders sometimes, that she daydreams, but she's not sure what about. Charline could never imagine the dark thoughts and unbearable flashes that push their way into Daphné's mind whenever she's least expecting it.

Happy people dancing in the pit. Everyone who came by the coat check to drop off their things. The young freckled woman who complained about the exorbitant prices. The guy wearing a baseball cap whose backpack weighed a ton. The teenage girl wrapped in a fuchsia scarf who had come back to get her phone from the pocket of her jean jacket. The couple who arrived late and headed into the concert holding hands, eager to enjoy the music together.

What happened to all those people? Did they get out unharmed, like her? Had they never left the Bataclan? Were they wounded? Did they die?

Daphné secretly pores over the victims' faces, feeling like she crossed paths with them, like she knows all of them, even though she realizes it's just an illusion. She's memorized all their names without even trying—they're stuck in her brain like stubborn splinters, so much a part of her now that she could recite them all in a single breath.

Those who weren't as lucky as she was.

From time to time, Charline notices her mother grabbing hold of a chair or some other piece of furniture, like she's about to fall, and the disconcerted little girl wonders if her mother has vertigo or vision problems. Daphné quickly catches her breath and reassures her daughter with a warm smile. So Charline convinces herself everything's fine, that there's nothing to worry about.

Daphné tries to push the memories away, to put them out of her mind, but they hang on determinedly, like hard water stains on an old bathtub. They've tucked themselves into the farthest corners of her brain, though sometimes the images that pop up seem so surreal that Daphné wonders if she imagined it all, made it all up, if maybe a few movie scenes have gotten mixed up with what she lived through. The flashes are full of bangs and screams, and they smell of fear and gunpowder, sweat and blood. She tells herself that maybe it's the price she's paying for being so happy to be alive, for the indecent joy that floods over her as soon as she opens her eyes each dawn. The price to pay for having survived, for managing to escape without saving anyone. Day after day, she sees the hand that reached out to her, the one she tried to help. She remembers pushing it away, how she left it to be trampled by the stampeding herd of fleeing concert-goers. She's obsessed with that hand, sees it everywhere, wants to yell, *Sorry!* and to implore, beg, and plead for forgiveness. Every night, the hand comes back without fail to haunt her dreams, but Daphné can never grab hold of it. She wants to, but her arms refuse to obey the orders from her brain; they stay stubbornly limp at her sides, useless and unmoving. Only her legs agree to act, running as far and as fast and for as long as possible.

Daphné saved herself and no one else. That's what haunts her, that's the terrible regret that eats away at her like aggressive gangrene. The night when she had to give up who she was to survive. She feels torn between the uncharacteristic zest for life she's been full of since November 13 and the dull, throbbing guilt that catches up with her whenever she feels a little too happy. She carries this burden she feels she deserves in silence. Her family and friends are constantly reaching out to comfort her with "We've been thinking of yous" and "I hope you're holding ups", flowers, phone calls, concerned looks, and hugs that exude both empathy and fear. Daphné can't muster the courage to ask them to stop, and doesn't dare explain that their attention hurts more than it helps. Because she's not worth so much love; she did nothing to deserve it. She's not a victim—she's alive, she's not even wounded, she hasn't got a scratch on her.

So when the hand appears before her eyes, when the panicked fingers try to grab her, to take her with them, Daphné steadies herself on the first thing her own hands can find. She holds on tight, so tight, to make sure the drowning fingers can't pull her down, to stay above the fray of bodies writhing like worms.

"Ouch, you're hurting me!"

When Daphné comes to, she sees Charline trying to push her hand away. She must have grabbed on to her daughter's shoulder when she didn't find any sturdy furniture nearby. She feels ashamed and lets go immediately. Charline rubs her collarbone, a frown on her face.

"I'm sorry, honey, I forgot myself for a second."

"I'm worried about you, Mom . . ."

"There's no reason to be worried, sweetheart! I'm doing great! Why don't we go to the park for a while?"

Charline nods and Daphné kisses her neck, eliciting a cheerful laugh.

Hand in hand, mother and daughter head out for a walk—Charline doesn't dare tell her mother that at eight, she's too old to hold hands. Instead, she holds her breath, taking advantage of her mother's eagerness, and convinces herself that these happy phases last much longer than the strange moments when her mother seems lost in an alternate reality.

When they reach the street, bundled up in their winter coats, Daphné asks Charline—with real enthusiasm—if she'd like to get waffles. "With a thick layer of chocolate and whipped cream on top? What do you think?" Her eyes sparkle and Charline agrees, reassured.

A few minutes later, she discreetly watches her mother as she chews on a bite of waffle with her eyes closed, savoring the sweet dessert. Daphné is focusing on the flavors flooding her mouth, not wanting to miss a thing. She can't bear the thought of gobbling down her food without paying attention anymore. She has these peaceful moments of respite, where her desires fuel her taste buds. "A platter of raw oysters and a glass of chardonnay, quick, quick," even if that means going out in her pajamas to find them. "Homemade shepherd's pie, quick, quick, let's peel the potatoes, you'll see, it's nothing like store bought, honey. White-chocolate-chip cookies, quick, quick, what do you mean we don't have any butter? Go knock on the neighbor's door and see if they have any, I'll cut the chocolate into chunks in the meantime." Daphné is rediscovering forgotten sensations and pleasures, her daughter exploring a world where frozen dinners and canned vegetables are but a vague memory.

But they're followed by unbearable moments when Daphné doesn't want anything, doesn't even want to eat. When any food at all is nauseating, when the tiniest pleasure plagues her with guilt. When simply knowing that others aren't eating anymore, that others are grieving, turns her stomach, sending waves of acid up her scorched esophagus. "I'm not hungry, sweetie. I think I ate too much at lunch." The little girl is no dupe, but she keeps quiet.

Charline lovingly wipes a smudge of whipped cream off her mother's nose with her index finger. She doubts a waffle counts as a real meal, but she convinces herself that it's better than nothing.

"Look, sweetheart, aren't the Christmas decorations beautiful?"

Daphné looks up at the lights strung up over the street, the same ones that were there last year, and every other year before that.

"They're gorgeous. Can you believe I never looked up to enjoy them before?"

Charline smiles sweetly at her mother's gaze, full of wonderment, glowing in the reflection of the bright stars hanging above them.

8

THÉO

Six months later

Ms. Rossignol has just noticed that today, Théo, whose desk is in the front row, isn't wearing the same shapeless sweatshirt she's gotten used to seeing him in since November. He seems to have exchanged the oversized navy-blue sweatshirt—he had to roll the sleeves at least three times to get them level with his wrists—for a sporty black windbreaker with green stripes.

The teacher doesn't say anything, of course, but wonders if maybe it's a positive sign. She's just twenty-four; this is her first year teaching, and she doesn't have much experience with mourning.

For six months, she's been doing her best to help the young boy, but she still hasn't managed to break the ice, to find a crack in the shell he's been hiding inside ever since he lost his dad. She never said anything about him coming to class day after day in an adult-sized sweatshirt—you didn't have to be a rocket scientist to figure out it must have been his father's, and that the boy had focused all his energy and grief on keeping it with him. Through a chat with his mom, Ms. Rossignol discovered that Théo only let it out of his sight to be washed every once in a long while. And the first time it had gone in the washer—two and a half months after that night—he had been hysterical. "Because the cherished sweatshirt wouldn't smell like his father anymore," his mother had mumbled with tears in her eyes. So his mother had bought him a bottle of Hugo Boss cologne, her ex-husband's scent, and Théo had taken to spraying the fragrance that brought back so many memories on his pillow before going to bed.

Théo doesn't talk much, and only speaks at all when spoken to. His grades are great, nothing to be said there, so Ms. Rossignol has simply been looking out for him, ready to pick him up if he should fall, both literally and figuratively.

She's noticed that he wistfully watches the clouds drifting by from his windowside desk all too often. That when his eyes lose focus, he's not really in the classroom anymore. That he's lost in his thoughts, in his memories, and that no one can make that any easier for him. That when she asks him to read aloud or recite his multiplication tables, he does it in a distant monotone. That when he's called to the board, he picks up the chalk and writes wordlessly, like a robot.

But she's also noticed that he perks up during art lessons, that he comes back to life when he uses his pencils and markers to draw extraordinary worlds and winged creatures born only of his imagination. Every now and again, a smile even tries to work its way onto his face, when he forgets and lets himself be happy, if only for a moment.

At recess, Ms. Rossignol keeps her eye on the little boy, to the point of ignoring the other students, who take advantage of this lack of supervision to tease each other and fight. She almost never lets Théo's little ash-blond head and big brown eyes out of sight. There are occasional days when he has fun with his classmates, playing soccer or trading marbles and popular stickers with the other children. He yells and horses around as much as the others. Those are the good days. The rest of the time, he sits alone on the only bench on the playground, and no one goes near him, as if they have somehow established an implicit agreement to let him be. He stares into space, and his eyes don't even track the ball rolling from one side of the playground to the other.

Today the teacher's walking on egg shells but thinks that maybe this activity will be a chance to shake the boy out of his stupor, to coax him out of mourning. Théo's mother told her a week ago that he refuses to talk about his father, that he's never said a single word about that night. Never. Not even with the child psychologist she'd taken him to see out of desperation. Théo had gone mute about the tragedy, and no one in the family knew if that was good or bad, if they needed to worry, or just let him grieve slowly, in his own way.

"Children, Father's Day is in a month, so I'd like us to spend one afternoon a week making gifts . . ."

She glances discreetly at Théo, who's fixated on the tall, unmoving maples outside.

"I've collected enough small glass jars for each of you to have one. The idea is to make shadow-projection candleholders using crepe paper and black construction paper."

The other students are excited, but Théo doesn't budge. The teacher quickly lays all the materials on her desk.

"The first step is to decide what shapes you want to draw on the black paper. You could choose people, trees, a castle, a heart—whatever you like!"

She shows them examples from pictures she printed at home last night, and the class lets out a round of enthralled oohs and aahs.

◆ ◆ ◆

The bell rings through the school, and the children hurry to leave their desks for the playground. Théo is about to stand up too, but the teacher motions him over to her desk. He reluctantly walks toward her.

"I know this isn't easy for you, Théo, so I wanted to talk to you about this candleholder project."

The boy waits for her to finish, staring at his fingernails, and Ms. Rossignol realizes he's not going to make this easy for her. She wants to find the right words and is so afraid of hurting him.

"Victor won't be able to give his present to his dad either," she begins hesitantly, "but last year he gave it to someone else in his family, an uncle, I think. Would *you* like to give yours to someone else you're close to?"

Feeling helpless, she wonders why no one's ever taught her how to handle a situation such as this, how to avoid making things worse. Maybe she should have kept quiet and let Théo come to her himself. Or talked to his mother first. But it's too late now, and when she sees flashes of fury in the boy's eyes, she concludes she's said something she shouldn't have.

"Victor's dad left! He left his wife to move to some other part of the country and live with someone else! Victor told me! That's nothing like me!"

"Yes, of course, I understand. I just meant that maybe you could—"

"That's nothing like my father! He didn't abandon me, okay? He didn't leave me, he didn't want to let go of my hand, I know that, I'm positive . . ."

Ms. Rossignol is distressed and disconcerted by this unexpected wave of anger. Théo's eyes fill with tears, as if the dam has finally been swept away.

"My father never would have left me! And I'm not going to give the candleholder to anyone else, because no one will ever be able to replace him!"

She mumbles again that she understands, hoping that the principal won't suddenly burst into her classroom. Théo goes quiet all of a sudden, wipes the trail of tears streaming down his cheeks, and sits back down at his desk without a sound. He focuses his gaze once more on the maples, and Ms. Rossignol can tell he's trying to escape back into his cocoon.

"What would you like to do, then?" she asks gently.

Without turning to look at her, the little boy replies drily, "I'm going to make a candleholder for my dad, like everybody else. I'm going to draw a fist with the pinky and the pointer finger in the air on the black construction paper. I know he'll like that. And on Father's Day, I'll take it to him."

"That's a great idea, Théo. I'm sorry I hurt your feelings . . ."

The boy reluctantly pulls his attention from the blue sky and looks at his teacher, who's fiddling nervously with her nails. His anger gives way to sadness, and he adopts a calmer tone.

"It's okay."

"It's not really okay. I want to help you, because I'm the adult, but apparently I'm only making things worse, and I'm truly sorry about that."

She realizes she's exposing her weaknesses, admitting that she's just as lost as he is, but she's been feeling so helpless for months, and honesty seems like the best option. He nods in agreement.

"This morning, when my mom dropped me off at school, a bus drove past. It slowed down right in front of me because the stop was right down the road. I saw my dad inside, leaning against the window, standing, holding on."

Ms. Rossignol frowns, but does not interrupt him.

"I was sure it was him, so I ran over. The bus had stopped and the doors were open, but when I looked through the window, he wasn't there anymore. I got on the bus while the driver sold a ticket to an old lady, but my dad was gone."

The teacher wants to hug the boy, but she holds back, sure that's the last thing he would want her to do.

"Every time I think I see him, it turns out not to be him. It's *never* him. But I still keep seeing him everywhere. In line at the grocery store, with the other parents waiting at the gate after school, on street corners, in the bleachers at the boxing gym, in the waiting room at the doctor's office . . . I look up and I see him. I blink and he's gone. It's either someone who doesn't even look like him, or nobody at all. I run after him, to see him again, but I can never catch up. It's so frustrating. It's like a giant ball of anger is growing inside me, little by little, made up of all the times when I'm disappointed, every time I get my hopes up for no reason. I almost feel like I'm suffocating by the end of the day, so I take my pillow and scream into it, pushing as hard as I can against my face so my mom won't hear. But the yelling doesn't make me feel better, it just tires me out. Sometimes I think it's so exhausting seeing Dad everywhere that I wish it would stop happening, but at the same time at least this way I won't forget about him. Because I'm so afraid of forgetting, of not remembering what his face looks like or the sound of his voice. I don't want him to disappear, to think I don't need him anymore. I don't want to lose him a second time . . ."

Théo stops short, nearly out of breath from opening up, and Ms. Rossignol offers a sad smile. She has no idea what to say, but she's also not sure the boy expects any reply at all.

The bell breaks the silence, and both of them jump.

"Do I have time to go to the bathroom?" asks Théo, shaken.

"Yes, but hurry up."

He springs out of his chair and dashes out of the room as the teacher begins laying the sheets of black construction paper on the students' desks.

9

LUCAS

Nine months later

"What can I get you, miss?"

The bakery employee's tone grows insistent as she notices that the line of customers behind Anouk will soon be out the door.

"Miss?"

The couple behind her puffs with impatience, and Anouk forces herself to decide.

"I'll have a small lemon tart and a mille-feuille, please."

Just as the annoyed woman behind the counter closes the pastry box, Anouk realizes she doesn't need the second dessert, but she can't change her order now. She hurries out of the bakery with her ribbon-bedecked box in hand.

Oh well, she'll eat both. Hers and Lucas's. For more than five years, she's bought the same two desserts for lunch every Sunday. Lucas used to tease her that it was the kind of habit people have after being married for decades, but it never kept him from being thrilled with his mille-feuille.

Old habits are hard to break.

He would carefully set aside the icing from the top of the cake to save for last, because it was his favorite part.

Is *his favorite part,* Anouk corrects herself sadly.

He would always turn on the GPS, but would never follow the directions the robotic voice spat at him because he knew better, had a foolproof shortcut, knew the other way would be jammed no matter the time of day.

He loved to end their conversations with corny expressions like *Relax, Max!* and *See you later, alligator!* He did it so often, Anouk found herself answering, *In a while, crocodile!* despite herself.

He was a poor sport, incapable of admitting that he hated to lose. "You're cheating! You don't even know the rules!" he would exclaim, pouting every time they played Risk or Monopoly. Anouk would sometimes let him win, just to spare them both his bad mood.

His favorite color was scarlet red, and Anouk had started wearing that color of lipstick because she knew he liked it.

As she walks up an avenue lined with bushes dried and browned by the August sun, Anouk wonders if Lucas still thinks about her. If he also finds himself overwhelmed with wistful memories that do more harm than good. If he also imagines what could have happened if she hadn't given him the concert tickets for their five-year anniversary. If he thinks everything could have been so different for them if not for that horrible night. Would they have stayed together, withstood the tests of time and day-to-day life? Would they have had a house full of children over the years . . . ?

They had certainly tried, no one could say otherwise. For months, they both fought to make it work, to put that night behind them and move forward, together. Lucas tried so hard to earn her forgiveness, and to forgive himself. Anouk tried to pretend that everything was all right, even though she knew something was broken.

He didn't realize that she had seen him get up, turn around, and flee that night. She'd seen him hesitate, instinctively weigh the pros and cons of doing so before *choosing* to leave, deciding to run away from the gunfire, away from her. Would she have done the same in his shoes? Maybe, likely. But that didn't keep her from thinking about it.

Anouk had stayed in that concert hall for hours, seeing and hearing everything. Fighting to keep at bay the anxiety attack that was threatening to overwhelm her, to ignore the feeling she was suffocating, about to explode, to staunch her feral desire to scream and release the terror from her body. She had held on to life, alone, huddled next to people she didn't know. She had never felt as vulnerable as she did lying on that cold, hard floor, never felt as fragile and helpless as she did listening to the bullets that could strike her at any time. At first, she kept saying in her head, *Please let me be okay, please God, let me be okay, let me get out of here unharmed . . .* , and then, as the salvoes of gunfire continued, seemingly unceasing, she had started to pray that a bullet would hit her head, or her heart: *Please let it kill me on impact, so I don't suffer, so I don't die slowly and painfully, just end it all without me realizing I'm the one they've hit this time . . . Let the damn thing be over with quickly, let it end this unbearable fear that's drowning me.* Because it had seemed clear that it would all end there that night, that there was no hope of escape. That nobody would escape. That no one would be left to tell the story, to bear witness.

Every time she had sensed movement around her, she had raised her head, despite it all, to see if it was Lucas trying to find her, coming to get her, checking all the bodies on the floor, hoping not to recognize her clothes or shoes among the dead.

And when it had all ended, she'd stood up without daring to believe it was true, and had exited the building with her hands on her head—still sure that a bullet would fell her, that she would slump to the ground, like all the others. The police had warned them not to look around, but she couldn't stop herself; she had to search for some sign of Lucas. She had known immediately that what she was seeing would stay burned on her retinas for the rest of her life, that she wouldn't be able to move past it, that it would haunt her forever, but she had to look for him. Had to make sure he wasn't lying there on the ground bleeding out. Had to listen, hoping not to hear the sound of his phone ringing in the deafening chorus of other cell phones ringing on the ground, with no one to answer them.

She had seen a body on the floor wearing a teal sweater like Lucas's. Had caught a glimpse of a guy with a similar haircut, unmoving in a dark puddle. A man in jeans, but who *doesn't* wear jeans? She had felt guilty about the relief that flooded her every time she realized it wasn't him. Because even if it wasn't him, it was still *somebody*. Somebody's boyfriend, father, or son, the person somebody was waiting for somewhere, without knowing. It wasn't him, but it could have been. It wasn't him, but on some level, they were all him.

She had stayed up all night waiting to find him, to know that he was alive somewhere. His voicemail kept picking up, as if the phone was turned off or the battery were dead. Jessica and Djibril held each other close while Anouk hoped against hope that her boyfriend would finally appear.

After giving a statement to a police officer who was just as dazed as she was, she had taken a taxi home. Nothing could have described her shock when she had found Lucas in the entryway taking off his coat. Trembling, Anouk had finally gotten the comfort she needed, nestled against his chest.

In the days that followed, Anouk came to accept that her boyfriend had fled without looking back, that even in the aftermath, he hadn't dared come close enough to the Bataclan to look for her, to make sure she was all right. Lucas's guilt grew, and she did nothing to stop it. He felt like a worthless coward for thinking only of himself, for being too scared to go back and find her. He cried in shame sometimes, when he thought she was sleeping. She understood why he'd done what he had, but she couldn't bring herself to accept it. She wanted to reassure him, but she couldn't.

Lucas had abandoned her that night. And even though it was understandable, justifiable, forgivable, and maybe even normal, Anouk couldn't quiet the little voice in her head singing the same refrain over and over again: *Lucas abandoned me. Lucas abandoned me. He fled and left me behind. He saved himself without a second thought and abandoned me. Abandoned abandoned abandoned.*

There was something definitive and irreversible about that choice. It was like she couldn't trust him anymore, would never feel safe with him again. She hated herself for feeling that way, but her mind couldn't convince her heart, couldn't wipe away the feeling that she had been betrayed, rejected.

Anouk had made it out of the massacre alive, but her life wasn't so important to her anymore, because she hadn't meant enough to the man she loved for him to come back for her.

So, day after day, week after week, their relationship had crumbled. Like rotting fruit—no one could stop it. Sadness, bitterness, and regret had crept in as the list of things left unsaid had grown longer—Lucas afraid to tell her he would have gone back for her if he could do it again, that he would turn around and look for her all night if he had to, in bars, in courtyards and buses, inside the goddamn concert hall where they'd lost each other forever; and Anouk unable to explain how embittered and anguished she felt knowing she had meant so little to the man she had been sure was the one.

Anouk had drifted away from Lucas, and he hadn't done anything to stop it since he felt he deserved it, as a sort of penance. He could have fought to keep her, fought for them, but he would have had to believe in himself at least a little, would have had to be strong enough to admit that he had done what he could that night.

Like everyone else.

The words they couldn't bring themselves to say were like a cancer relentlessly attacking each of their organs. They thought that talking would only make it hurt more, that it was better for each of them to try to come back up to the surface on their own, and that then they could be together again, like *before*. At barely twenty-five years old, they were too young for this kind of daily tragedy. They were at an age where, when things aren't going so well, you break up without a fight because there's time, so much time to have something else with someone else.

So when the cancerous silence triumphed over their bodies, their hearts stopped fighting, deprived of oxygen and compassion. All that was left was affection and a bittersweet nostalgia that were no longer enough. Without a word, without a sound, their hearts stopped beating in the same rhythm, until the oppressive silence became unbearable, choking the life out of them both, like an ungrateful, overfed snake.

One spring morning, Lucas finally read in Anouk's gray eyes flecked with gold that it was over. He looked down at his feet, resigned to it. "I screwed everything up," he whispered, unable to speak any louder. Without answering, because of the sobs threatening to escape her chest, Anouk helped him pack his things. He took only the bare minimum, not wanting to bring a bunch of stuff with him that would always remind him of her and of their failed relationship. Before leaving their home for the last time, he'd quietly sung the words to the song she used to love so much, "I would beg you if I thought it would make you stay," and she had looked away, without a word.

In the stairwell, Lucas had thought about all the times when Anouk took him on endless shopping trips. *Are you sure this dress looks good on me? Is the color right?* All the times he had sighed and answered that everything always looked perfect on her. All the times she had rolled her eyes in response to syrupy-sweet compliments.

In the now-silent apartment, Anouk had thought about all the times Lucas went out of his way to send postcards to his parents during their vacations. All the times she made fun of his obsession, which she thought old-fashioned. All the times he proudly showed her the glossy card on his parents' refrigerator—*It makes them so happy, see?*

That day, Lucas would have given anything for a few hours shopping with Anouk, and she would have done the same to go back to their last vacation, in the summer of 2015, back to the sweltering streets of Barcelona to spend the entire afternoon going from shop to shop to find just the right postcard for Lucas's parents.

Anouk had watched as he exited the building and walked to his car in the pouring rain, and it occurred to her, with a heavy heart, that this deluge would have been the perfect backdrop for a Hollywood kiss. That in a romantic comedy, it wouldn't have been too late, that there's always hope for the happy ending everyone wants, whether it seems realistic or incredibly far-fetched. In a movie, there would have been a close-up of her tear-rimmed eyes, a fixed moment in time before she rushed down the stairs to reunite with Lucas in the middle of the street. He would have taken her in his arms, hastily dropping the heavy box he was carrying, and they would have kissed passionately, not at all bothered by the rain whipping at them or their soaked clothes. Cars would have had to stop for the young love-struck couple, blocking the road without even realizing it. They wouldn't have heard the concert of horns beeping around them, nor seen passersby slow to watch their moving embrace from beneath their umbrellas. They would have been alone in another world—together.

But Anouk had simply watched as the red Renault Clio's lights turned on, and her gaze followed the car distractedly until it was out of sight.

Because in real life, sometimes it is too late. And nobody is strong enough to change that.

When she gets home, Anouk gently opens the pastry box and removes the top layer of icing from the mille-feuille. After enjoying the pastry cream and puff pastry, she runs her finger over the smooth, shiny surface of the icing Lucas loved so much.

Out of nowhere, she bursts into tears, which leave winding paths on the icing where they fall. As she sits there alone in her kitchen, her crying turns into desperate sobs and hiccups, because no one's there to take her in their arms anymore.

10

Romane

A year later

Romane conscientiously hangs the huge frame on the wall of the little guest room, which is full of piles of laundry waiting to be folded and books hoping to somehow find a spot in the jam-packed Ikea bookcase.

Léopold watches as she takes a few steps back to evaluate her handiwork. Romane has her black hair up in a messy bun held in place by a colored pencil, with strands dangling around her temples.

"It's nice, right?" she asks, unsure.

"It's perfect." Léopold reassures her with a smile.

"But . . . is it a good idea to hang it here?"

"It's a great idea," he says as he walks over and takes her in his arms.

Together they contemplate the picture on the wall, without speaking. The only sound is the cooing of the pigeons on the roof of their old building, wafting in through their top-floor windows. Romane strokes Léopold's forearm without thinking, her index finger running over the eight tattooed tentacles she now knows by heart, having admired and traced them one by one. There's a tiny numeral hidden within each of them, tucked in among the suction cups, so that only the most discerning or practiced eye can see them. Eight numbers in all, which together make up the date November 13, 2015.

The day they met.

Because just over a year ago, the couple met under circumstances that neither of them will ever forget. They could have never seen each other again, if Léopold hadn't thought to give her his number, and if Romane hadn't worked up the courage to call him the next week. If they hadn't had such a visceral connection, such a fervent need to be together to come back up to the surface, back to reality. If they hadn't locked eyes for what seemed like an eternity, if he hadn't held on by imagining the life he could have with the pretty girl across the way, if she hadn't stayed afloat by silently explaining how to make macarons.

They could have never seen each other again, but they did.

They could have had nothing to say to one another, but they've never needed words to communicate. And silence doesn't scare either of them, after living through endless hours of blaring Kalashnikov volleys.

Léopold knows that the reason they've been together ever since, the reason they've hardly been apart since last November is because of—or thanks to—the connection they forged that night. Alex, Tiago, and Sylvain all lived through the same thing, of course. And Adèle too. But they didn't wait it out *with* someone, didn't share the strange combination of internal strife and resignation to death, which had seemed so imminent. They didn't hope or hold on *together*.

Over the next weeks, then months, they leaned on each other to regain their zest for life, to fight the irrational fear they had that someone was coming for them, that it would happen again. Romane didn't have to explain to him why she suddenly stopped midaction sometimes, as the water from the faucet ran over her hands, because he always knew exactly what it reminded her of. And Léopold didn't have to justify his obsession with making sure her phone was on silent—at the movies and everywhere else. When they both froze in unison at the sound of a distant ambulance siren or a car backfiring, neither of them felt the need to offer an explanation.

It took a lot of patience, empathy, affection, and especially love. A lot of love.

When people ask them how they met, Léopold and Romane simply answer, "At a concert," with a smile, pleased with the banality of their answer, the way it never elicits any further questions or curiosity. It's not that they want to lie or hide the truth, but they feel there's no point bringing it up with people who would never be able to understand anyway. They've had enough compassionate faces, pity-filled looks, and comforting words to last a lifetime. Of course both of them know they'll never be able to erase what happened that night from their memories, that the best-case scenario is that the images will fade, the colors and sounds become less vivid, less violent, less omnipresent. They can only hope to get used to it, to adapt to them, to find a way to hide them deep down, far from others.

They met at a concert, like hundreds of other *normal* couples. People imagine the dim lights, shy smiles, hands brushing against one another, and everyone finds it sweet. Romane and Léopold don't mind the fact that the scene isn't quite right, since the shared gaze that brought them together for hours was exactly that: sweet.

They met at a concert, and have continued to go see their favorite bands play, dancing and singing in rhythm to the songs they enjoy. Romane and Léopold don't always have the same taste, but neither one of them would ever imagine going to a concert without the other. Together, always. Out of love, and out of superstition. Romane has made sure to be in the audience at every one of Léopold's concerts for the past year, in the front row no matter what, her eyes focused on the frenzied drummer. At first, she had to force herself, confront her fears, but together they repeat the same thing every time, a kind of mantra that keeps them moving forward: *We can't stop living*. And they didn't, not even when they sometimes felt like the simple things—eating, going out, talking, sleeping, and even breathing—took all their strength and energy, like they had to relearn how to do it all.

They met at an unfinished concert, so when the Eagles of Death Metal announced their return to the stage in Paris, at the Olympia this time, exactly three months and three days after November 13, Léopold and Romane didn't even need to discuss it to know they'd be going, whether or not they really wanted to. Romane thought of the concert as a sort of pilgrimage, an homage—she felt like she *had* to go, for all the people who wouldn't be there, for the part of herself she had lost that night. Attending the concert would be like an act of resistance, proof that they would never forget. She hoped she might find herself again there, that it might be a good way to finally get some *closure*. She saw the second concert as a symbolic ending, even though she knew it wouldn't put a stop to everything, that her wounds wouldn't miraculously disappear. She hoped, at best, that it would help them heal, help the scars fade.

As they waited in line on Boulevard des Capucines, they noticed just how many people were there on crutches or in wheelchairs, but they didn't say a word. They suddenly felt so lucky, guilty that their own wounds were invisible, that the only damage they had sustained was on the *inside*. Just a few yards away, a horde of journalists, video cameras, and microphones was on the lookout for moving personal accounts, a few tears, or the slightest sign of fear. Léopold didn't enjoy feeling like a circus act. He instinctively squeezed Romane's hand a little tighter.

He didn't know what to expect that night. Would the music be enough to lift the weight that had been pressing down on his chest for the past three months? He decided it was better not to get his hopes up. Without thinking, he and Romane took their places in the same spot as the first concert, even though it wasn't the same venue. As if they'd really come to *finish* the concert. Léopold didn't recognize anyone around him, and a wave of sadness suddenly washed over him. As if he'd been expecting a family reunion, only to realize he'd made a mistake, that despite their shared ordeal, strangers were still strangers. He reveled in the hugs from his friends when they made their way to him and Romane, and they waited anxiously together for the band to come on stage.

When Jesse Hughes finally appeared, with the carefree melody of "Il est cinq heures, Paris s'éveille" playing in the background, he was met with such thunderous applause and boisterous shouting, so full of life, that it left him speechless. He just stood there, as if looking at each of them one by one. Léopold could feel his stomach writhing, his throat tighten with all the emotions trying to escape. The hairs on his arms stood up, as if someone had pressed rewind and the past three months had disappeared for a split second. The singer blew kisses, raised his fists in the air, ran his fingers through his hair with a trembling hand, then brought his hands, palms touching, to his face, unable to express how overwhelmed with emotion he felt to see all the people who'd found the courage to come back.

With a lump in her throat, Romane watched as Hughes's bright-red suspenders rose and fell in time to his breathing, visibly ragged with emotion. At that exact moment, she would have sworn that the entire audience felt an intense and indescribable wave rush over them, a combination of joy, grief, thankfulness, and love. The feeling that they all belonged to something bigger, that they were united, sharing in the moment, as one. Then the singer's tattooed arms pulled the strap of his white guitar over his head, and the much-awaited—and dreaded—concert finally began.

The music didn't erase all their pain, but for a few hours, amid all the other tortured souls in the room, their wounds didn't seem so deep, so insurmountable, so unbearable. None of the concert-goers wanted

November 13 to become their identity, to sum up who they were for the rest of their lives, and for a fleeting moment that night, they let themselves sing, yell, and dance, despite their sadness and grief, despite the knowledge that nothing would ever be like before again.

Just after ten o'clock, Léopold glanced discreetly at his cell phone, and couldn't help but feel incredibly relieved. Nothing had interrupted the music, and they were still alive. They would make it out of this concert hall unscathed—almost.

Afterward, everyday life quickly took over, but neither of them has forgotten the intense feelings they shared with the crowd, with the group that night. The sudden fragile feeling that they would pick themselves up again and move forward, that one day they would no longer feel like they were riding the wake of that terrible, fateful night, but that they were truly living again.

Léopold places his hands on Romane's stomach and rests his head in the crook of her neck.

"Do you think it's a boy or a girl?" he asks.

"If it's a boy, we could call him Charles," she says, caressing his stubbly cheek, her eyes glued to the frame she's just hung on the wall.

"Let's hope it's a girl, then," murmurs Léopold before taking an elbow to the side and bursting into laughter.

On the wall, in what will be a nursery a few months from now, a crowd of raised heads look toward a mustachioed singer going all out on the Bataclan stage, determined to give his fans the best concert of their lives. Some of them are resting their elbows on the crowd barricade in the front row, thrilled to be as close to the band as possible. Others, in the balcony, are standing, unable to stay seated while listening to such a vibrant beat, maybe even secretly jealous of the lucky ones dancing down in the pit.

In the warm glow of the blinding spotlights, all their faces are smiling, happy to be there, carefree.

Radiant.

On the right-hand side of the picture, near the front row, Léopold is there, raising his phone energetically into the air so his friend, who was disappointed not to be there, can listen in.

And all the others are there too.

AFTERWORD

November 13, 2015

I pored over the faces of the human beings who were massacred that night for no reason at all—dozens, maybe even hundreds of times. So many times that I started to feel like I knew them all, had loved them all. I was grieving for them all despite the fact that I had never even met a single one of them.

Again and again, I watched the looped footage of the dozens of dark figures fleeing the Bataclan followed by echoing bursts of gunfire. Each and every time, I was left stunned. Paralyzed, like I had been on a certain September 11, when I had seen two planes the size of flies crash into two towering skyscrapers. *It can't be real.* I was a teenager in 2001; I was an adult in 2015. The emotions were the same. Only this time, there was also the sadness of wondering what kind of world our children would grow up in and how we'd ever be able to explain some people's senseless violence and others' powerlessness to prevent it.

I lost interest in everything else for weeks. With tears in the corners of my eyes and my stomach clenched in rage, I watched the news and browsed the Internet, unable to think about anything other than that night.

I was embarrassed about the depth of my feelings. I felt like my grief and shock were somehow misplaced, almost indecent, in the face of all those who had been there, those who had lost a loved one, those who would be traumatized by what they had been through for who knew how long.

Despite myself, time stopped for me on November 13. I couldn't help but feel like the rest of the world hadn't waited long enough to return to its usual hustle and bustle.

In December, I went to pay my respects outside the Bataclan and the terraces of the Parisian cafés that had been attacked. I was filled with a fathomless emptiness when I saw all the wilted flowers, faded drawings, letters, and candles doing their best to withstand the wind.

As I write these lines, I can almost smell the warm wax again—such an unusual scent in the city streets. The smell of all the birthdays we have been blessed to celebrate over the course of our lives. Our own, and those of our families and friends. The scent of warm wax has so often been synonymous with happiness.

I didn't want to write this book. Transposing every image and idea into words was grueling, and each word was painful to distill. I was compelled to write it, obliged to put everything else aside during the weeks it poured out of me. I naïvely believed that once the sentences had run their course through me, my inner turmoil would subside. But the opposite happened.

When I woke up on the morning of November 14 and learned what had happened, and later as I watched and read witness statements scattered all over the Web, I had a sudden suffocating feeling that the victims had been just like me. They were my generation.

A generation that has only known war through history books or from so far away that it seems unreal, intangible. A generation that goes to rock concerts and enjoys the simple pleasures of gathering together—in a kind of communion—with strangers, all swaying in rhythm to the same music. A generation that likes to have drinks at a sidewalk café to take advantage of the final days of crisp fall weather.

A generation that has been taught that so many things are dangerous or risky. Taught to fear AIDS, economic crises, global warming, junk food, cigarettes, cancer, unemployment, Wi-Fi waves, and so much more.

A generation whose parents let them run around outside, but who will never let their own children do the same. Too dangerous, too risky.

A generation devoid of illusions, but so very full of dreams.

A generation that can now add terrorism to the list of things to fear, to the list of things we must fight and stand tall against.

Because that's who we are, that's who they were: a generation of fighters. A generation that should be afraid of everything, but refuses to be afraid of anything.

For a host of other indescribable reasons, they were us.

And because they were us, I had to imagine their story, their fate, had to turn them into characters. I didn't re-create them; I invented them. I didn't reconstruct them or re-create them through the painstaking process of collecting information from various sources, checked and rechecked for accuracy. I didn't want to rummage through the private lives of real people—I would neither know how nor be able to do it. Besides, it's not my job; I'm not a journalist. I invented them insofar as they came pouring out of me, of their own volition, because in a way they are me, and us too. Maybe you'll recognize yourself in one of them, as you could have recognized yourself in any of the men and women who were at the Bataclan that night.

All the characters in this book are fictional. They're not real, but they are, I hope, true. This book explores the intermingled fates of ten imagined people and their loved ones. Ten characters who are perhaps even truer than life, ten people I so wish I had been able to save.

I wasn't at the Bataclan with them on November 13, 2015. Their story is neither a personal account nor an essay. It's not exactly a novel, though, either; it is too heavily based on reality for that.

It is quite simply an attempt—most likely clumsy and perhaps illegitimate, but deeply sincere and absolutely inevitable—to make something bright flow from the darkness. I believe that is writing's role: to reinvent reality, exorcise it and transcend it, to make it less terrifyingly dark, more approachable. I hope that those who read this book will understand, that my words will bring something to the world. I wrote this text when feelings were running high, before our memories and feelings could fade, while they were still violent and omnipresent.

One Night in November is my tribute to the victims and their loved ones. More than anything else, however, it's a call to remember, because we will forget soon, too soon; we'll move on to other things, like we always do. It's the candle I humbly light, with the hope that it will withstand the wind and the passage of time.

I hope that my words will do some good. That my characters are a worthy tribute to all the victims of November 13, 2015.

To those who didn't survive, and to those who continue to fight to live their lives.

May we never forget.

❖ ❖ ❖

Contact information: amelie.antoine.auteur@gmail.com
Facebook: www.facebook.com/AmelieAtn

ACKNOWLEDGMENTS

I'd like to thank Mathieu for supporting me as I wrote this arduous text. Thank you for standing by me, even when you feared that the words would pull me under rather than soothe me.

My thanks also go out to my father for his reaction upon reading *One Night in November*, which made me realize the emotions others might have in response to this difficult novel.

I'd also like to thank my first readers, before publication: Solène, Mélanie, Cyril, Florence, Isabelle, and Patrick. Thank you for going down the rabbit hole with me; thank you for believing in this book, which is so important to me.

Thank you to the team at Amazon Kindle Direct Publishing France, for getting behind my second novel, even though it wasn't published under my name at first. Thank you, Éric and Bérénice, as always, for your patience and dedication to helping independent authors.

I'd also like to thank Amazon Publishing for reading *Au nom de quoi* and offering to publish an English translation. Thank you to Maren Baudet-Lackner for translating this text—I wouldn't have been comfortable giving it to anyone else!

And, since I'm an incorrigible optimist, thanks in advance to the French publisher who may one day have the courage and audacity to bring this novel to bookstores.

Finally, thank you, readers, for picking up *One Night in November* and sharing your time with Abigaëlle, Philippe, Sofiane, Bastien, Léopold, Margot, Daphné, Théo, Lucas, and Romane.

If this text has touched you, please talk about it with your friends, face-to-face or via social media, and review it online. And please don't hesitate to contact me—you can't imagine how much your messages help fuel my desire to write.

ABOUT THE AUTHOR

Amélie Antoine's bestselling debut novel, *Interference*, was an immediate success when it was released in France, winning the first *Prix Amazon de l'auto-édition* (Amazon France Self-Publishing Prize) for best self-published e-book. In 2011, she published her memoir, *Combien de temps. One Night in November*, written as "a call to remember," is her second novel. Antoine lives in northern France with her husband and two children.

ABOUT THE TRANSLATOR

Maren Baudet-Lackner grew up in New Mexico. After earning a bachelor's degree from Tulane University in New Orleans, a master's in French literature from the Sorbonne, and a master of philosophy degree in the same subject from Yale, she moved to Paris, where she lives with her husband and children. She has translated several works from the French, including Amélie Antoine's first novel, *Interference*, the novel *It's Never Too Late* by Chris Costantini, and the nineteenth-century memoir *The Chronicles of the Forest of Sauvagnac* by the Count of Saint-Aulaire.